GREGORY, MAW, and the MEAN ONE

GREGORY, MAW, and the MEAN ONE

by David Gifaldi

Decorations by
Andrew Glass

CLARION BOOKS

NEW YORK

Clarion Books
a Houghton Mifflin Company imprint
215 Park Avenue South, New York, NY 10003
Text copyright © 1992 by David Gifaldi
Decorations copyright © 1992 by Andrew Glass

Printed in the U.S.A.

Library of Congress Cataloging-in-Publication Data
Gifaldi, David.
Gregory, Maw, and the Mean One / by David Gifaldi.
p. cm.
Summary: In 1906, when the foul-tempered Mean One threatens a
small Western town, a young boy and the crow that raised him take
the varmint back in time to uncover the cause of
his rotten disposition.
ISBN 0-395-60821-X
[1. Humorous stories. 2. Behavior — Fiction. 3. West (U.S.) — Fiction.
4. Time travel — Fiction.] I. Title.
PZ7.G3625Gr 1992
[Fic] — dc20   91-34163
                                         CIP
                                          AC
BP 10 9 8 7 6 5 4 3 2 1

For Paul and Mark,
'cause Maw wishes it so

CONTENTS

GREGORY, MAW, and the MEAN ONE

1. A Hot Day

Sharpesville was in the midst of a heat spell the day the Mean One rode into town. By noon the flies had lost their buzz. Blistered and crazed, they flung themselves headlong into post or pane. Some simply exploded in midair . . . *tick, tick.* Like corn popping on a hot griddle. *Tick, tick, tick.*

The townsfolk sat hugging the shade in front of the shops along Main Street. The older ones — like Marsh Gibbons, whose lungs weren't what they used to be — had to chop the thick air with their hands just so they could breathe. Others blew through their lips before taking a breath, as if trying to cool a bowl of scalding soup.

"Hot."

"Yep."

"Too hot."

"Yep."

"Hotter than hot."

"Mercy!"

That was about the extent of conversation. *Tick-tick, chop-chop, whoo-whoo.*

Sy Stewart, the barber, was the first to notice the smell. It sent a jolt through his body and made his eyes cross. Millie Halverson, who ran the dry goods store, thought the man was having a seizure. "My . . . Sy," she murmured through cracked lips. Then she, too, had to cross her eyes.

That's the thing about meanness. It stinks something awful, and the townsfolk could smell trouble even though it was still some distance away. Each was aware that such a smell could come only from the Mean One. And though their instinct was to run, they knew there was no hiding from the dreaded M.O.

"Doomed," said Sy.

"Pickled," said Millie.

Marsh Gibbons' hands were a blur as they splintered the air in front of his face. "G-goners," he said with a gasp.

Fiona Meechum's fleshy lower lip trembled at such a forecast. Large and overly fond of sweets, Fiona wanted to kick herself for not finishing off last night's huckleberry pie when she had the chance.

"Dang it, anyhow," she said. Then she slapped her brow as if stung by a bee. "Omigosh! The younguns!"

You can't blame the parents for having momentarily forgotten their little darlings. It was hot, after all, and "out of sight, out of mind" applied back then even as it does today. Fiona's thwacking reminder started a hollering as fierce as any cattle roundup.

"Gertie! Philip! Lucy!"

"Ho, Fritz! Chester! Emma!"

"Herbert — you scamp — don't let me have to call a second time."

"Prudence! Willie! Mirabell!"

In fact, the children's keen young sniffers had picked up the smell long before the adults. It was just that, like all children, they liked to play far from the watchful eyes of parents and tattling grammas. They had already dropped from trees and scrabbled from hideouts, and were leaving a trail of dolls, jump ropes, and slingshots behind them when they heard their names called.

"The Mean One! The Mean One!" they yelled as they stampeded into town with spines tingling and eyes ballooned with fear. Sy and Millie directed the older ones to shimmy under the boardwalk for cover. Mothers quickly seized the youngest, tucking them beneath their skirts.

Little Gert, not quite four and Fiona's pride and joy, was the last to arrive. She stood barefoot, bow-legged, and on the verge of tears before the assemblage.

"Mama," she said, holding her bottom. "I think I forgot again."

"Oh, you poor, poor child!" Fiona cried. "That smell isn't you." And she swept up Little Gert into her ample arms and nearly squeezed the tiny girl to death before dropping her into the empty rain barrel outside Ferguson's Land Office.

So it was that the heat and the Mean One brought together all but two of the residents of Sharpesville on that fateful August afternoon.

"We'll stick together to the end," said Millie.

"All for one, and one for all," said Sy.

"Amen," said the preacher, clasping his Bible tighter and looking heavenward. "Nice knowin' y'all," he added.

Then they waited, coughing and pinching their noses, their scorched heads filled with the horrible stories they had heard.

2. The Stories

What filled the heads of Millie, Sy, Marsh, and the others just then wasn't pretty. For the Mean One had a reputation as big and ghastly as his seven-foot frame. For over a decade he had terrorized the towns and settlements along the Pustulli River. It is said that he once heaved a horse sixty feet through a hotel window — though whether he took a full windup or let the horse fly from a stretch position is still hotly debated.

Regardless, if you know horses you know they don't like to be heaved. They like to keep their hooves flat on the ground. That's just the way of it. And, well, let's face it, a hotel window has never asked to be smashed. (Windows are rather shy and nontalkative as a whole.)

So why does a person toss a horse sixty feet through a hotel window? Because he's ornery and spiteful and cruel, that's why. And that, in a nutshell, sums up the Mean One's reputation.

Word had it that in Vicksburg the Mean One had punched his way straight through a brick wall to get at the sheriff. Seems the sheriff, a man named Zimm, had boasted that if the Mean One thought he could waltz into Vicksburg looking for trouble, it would be his last dance.

The sheriff is buried in four plots in the town's cemetery. He was buried in one plot at first. But then parts of him kept being discovered on the outskirts of town, and rather than deal with the messiness of digging up the first grave, the townspeople had simply dug a fresh one, then another, and another. If you visit the cemetery, you can read the tombstone for yourself:

HERE LIES SHERIFF ZIMM
AND THERE AND THERE AND THERE.
A BRAVE MAN, A STUPID MAN
WHO NEVER KNEW WHAT HIT 'IM.

It's a sure bet that Amos Fletcher, Sharpesville's own illustrious sheriff, was recalling this very event as the Mean One's stench continued to roll down Main Street that day. Amos reached for the silver star on his chest and ripped it clean off his shirt. The badge went sailing — all eyes following its arc — and kicked up a fountain of dust as it landed in front of the livery stables across the way.

"Ain't no sheriff," Amos said. "Never was."

Seeing the badge of the law lying facedown in the dusty street brought new shudders of fear to Fiona and the other parents in the crowd. For that was another thing about the Mean One. He particularly disliked children. Didn't matter if they were fat or thin, tall or short, rosy cheeked or pimpled. He hated them all.

Once the Mean One paid a surprise visit to the children of Hulberton. It was the time of year between fall and winter, when children often forget to dress warmly enough. For days the town's parents had pleaded with their little ones.

"Your long johns," they'd say.

"You'll need a coat."

"It's freezing out there!"

"You'll catch your death."

And so forth.

But did the children listen? No! And lickety-split they all caught colds. Unfortunately, the colds were not the feverish, stay-at-home kind. And one night the children snuck away from their houses to play near the woods on the edge of town. They played Simon says and hide-and-go-seek in the evening twilight, sniffling and snuffling and sharing one another's germs, having a grand time.

With their noses stuffed, the children never noticed the Mean One's smell. Within the woods was an old shack. Since no one lived there, the children were surprised to see a light shining through the shack's worn lumber. Curious, they knocked on the door. The light went out and the door creaked open . . . and down dropped the Mean One from the loft above, yelling like a stuck pig, right in front of their faces.

The children's eyes spun circles in their heads and their hair shot up as if lightning struck. They took off through the woods screaming for their mamas, running into patches of stinging nettles freshly prickered. When they got home, they had to take baths to soothe their burning skin. *Baths!* And it wasn't even Saturday.

In Medford, the Mean One stuffed the newly hired schoolmaster, a Mr. Jonathan Petri, halfway up the schoolhouse chimney.

"Welcome, you vile little know-nothings," he said when the children arrived with their books and slates. "Repeat after me: The Earth is flat. The moon is made of moldy cheese. And birds fly north for the winter." He made them say this over and over while he scraped his long hard nails back and forth across the front blackboard.

At recess, he took all their lunches and made them eat spinach-and-mud sandwiches instead. There were wormy apples for dessert. And slimy, two-year-old pickle brine to wash it all down.

That night the children's parents asked them to recite their lessons. "The Earth is flat," the children said. "The moon is made of moldy cheese. And birds fly north for winter." They were each rewarded by being sent to bed early for not paying attention in class. For the Mean One it was the perfect ending to a perfect day.

There were other stories that the citizens of Sharpesville could have recalled. Plenty. But there wasn't time. For suddenly Main Street was choked by a wind so hot and foul that the buildings bubbled their paint as though stricken with poison ivy. Those with straight hair found themselves with curls. Curls spun out into straight. Noses twitched. Eyes watered. Cats yowled. Under the boardwalk, the children followed the lead of their dogs and quickly scraped holes in the dirt to bury their faces.

All who dared turned toward the north end of town.

Clip-clop. Clip-clop.

The Mean One! Bearded and filthy. Sitting atop the biggest horse anyone had ever seen.

Three swift boot kicks and the town's welcome sign was a pile of shattered kindling.

A single shove and the public privy was down for the count — a half-used Sears catalogue flying out from its moon-shaped airhole.

Then gunfire. So loud it rattled the gold fillings in Fiona's mouth. The few flies who hadn't yet ticked off were shot down in a hail of bullets as two forty-fives peppered the sky.

"ANYBODY HOME?" came the booming, full-of-nasty voice through the guns' swirling smoke.

It was then that Little Gert, who had become quite bored with the inside of her rain barrel, found the knothole below the barrel's rim. The knothole faced south, so Little Gert's view was not of the Mean One. What Gertie saw approaching still quite small in the distance was a boy. A happy, lanky, whistling, all-is-right-with-the-world boy. Gertie recognized the boy at once as one of her bestest friends. And she yelled, "GEGGIE!"

All heads swiveled to the town's south end.

"Not today," Millie said with a groan. "Oh, Gregory . . . why, oh why did you choose today?"

"The Lord giveth and the Lord taketh away," mumbled the preacher.

Sy sighed.

Marsh Gibbons's hands could have sliced and diced a twenty-pound sack of potatoes.

"Bad timing, Geggie," he said.

3. Gregory and Maw

Bad timing, all right. But how was Gregory to know? He was simply on his way to town to do some trading and to say how-do? to his new friends.

Gregory had settled a mile downstream from Sharpesville only the previous spring. He lived alone. 'Cept for Maw. He and Maw had tacked together a nice little place for themselves using drift boards they found along the bank. Maw had held the nails at the ready as Gregory hammered. She could hold six nails in her beak at a time. Maw was a crow. The only mother Gregory had ever known.

How Gregory and Maw came upon each other is like this. Maw lived up around Paducah. Kentucky born and raised. She flew off one morning on her usual breakfast hunt. When she returned, there was Gregory. In her nest. A boy baby. Saying *goo-goo* and *gaa-gaa*, and other mysterious stuff. You can imagine Maw's surprise. Below stood a young woman. "Pretty," Maw told Gregory when he was old enough to understand. "With a nice head of black hair."

The woman asked Maw to look after her baby for a while. "Till the feudin's over," she said. "Buckshot flyin' every which way. Ain't healthy for a newborn. I'll be back when I can. Gregory's such a good, happy babe. I love him to pieces."

Maw could understand. She was just then loving the last few pieces of a plump breakfast worm as they slid in a ball down her throat.

Whatever happened, happened. The young woman never returned. Maw did her best under the circumstances. She brought Gregory all the seeds and berries she could find. She tried worms once. But Gregory spit them out. "Never met a vegetarian before," Maw thought. But she was open-minded concerning religion, and she never pressed the issue.

At night Maw cuddled close to Gregory and kept him warm with the down of her feathers. Gregory would sigh and *goo* at her. "You're a good, happy babe," Maw said. "Though you grow at a fearsome rate."

It was true. Gregory stretched Maw's nest for

all it was worth. Maw kept waiting for him to sprout feathers and a decent pair of wings, but he never did. She gave him lessons in wing flapping nonetheless, and Gregory moved his arms in imitation. Finally, she could see no other way. She gave him a push. Gregory did his best flapping. But of course boy babies can't fly. And he dropped like a stone. Luckily, Maw had fixed up a nice cushion of Kentucky bluegrass below. And Gregory landed with a thump, only slightly dazed.

"Didn't think so," Maw said. "But it was worth a try. I love you even if you can't fly." Gregory poked his fingers in her eyes to show he felt the same.

Even Maw's cuddling couldn't keep Gregory warm when the weather turned. She was forced to thievery, pulling woolen baby outfits and blankets from every clothesline in Paducah (though she never took twice from the same line). She swiped bonnets too — the bigger the better, since it was a strain for her to pull them over Gregory's head, bald though he was.

At twleve months Gregory was already fluent in Crow. He leaned to speak People from listening to the children and parents who frequented the pond that lay nearby. The people most often came on weekends, laughing and shouting and carrying baskets of food.

The first word Gregory ever spoke was *Yippee!* — which is what most of the children said when they threw off their clothes and jumped in the pond. Soon he was saying such phrases as *Don't drown your sister, He hit me first,* and *Somebody wants a lickin'.* He also learned to say *Pass the mayo* and *I could eat a horse.*

Maw learned, too. Though she preferred the more truthful language of caws and head-bobbing that was Crow. "Never yet seen anyone eat a horse," she said. "Why lie about it?"

When Gregory was old enough, he and Maw took to the open road. "The world is meant to be seen," Maw said. She snapped off a long blade of grass and pushed it toward Gregory. "Here, stick this between your teeth."

"How come?" asked Gregory.

"You ever seen a traveler without one?"

"No."

"Well, there you have it. Knew I shouldn't have waited so long. You've got a lot to learn. Let's go."

Maw perched on Gregory's shoulder or flew before him as they traveled. They were good together. Good at exploring and finding food. Good at singing and laughing and being happy. Once they saw some children sitting beneath a tree. One of the children was moving her finger across a book and saying stuff like "My . . . Grandma . . . what big ears you have."

"Why's she moving her finger and eyes like that?" Gregory asked.

"Beats me," Maw said. "I don't even see a grandma."

The girl stopped talking, and the children began teasing and chasing one another. They forgot all about the book, and when they left, Gregory picked it up. "It's got scratches on it," he said.

"Footprints," said Maw. She hopped over the pages, twisting her ankles this way and that. "Ain't crow's feet, that's for sure. Too small."

"They mean something," Gregory said. "Got to." And he tucked the book under his shirt.

That night, when Gregory and Maw were looking for a good place to bed down, they came upon a man sitting on the steps of a bright-blue wagon. The man had slicked-down hair and a moustache almost as wide as Maw's wingspan.

"There's them scratches again," Gregory said.

The man jumped up in alarm. "Somebody been vandalizin' my wagon? Where? I don't see nothin'."

"There," said Gregory.

"Why, them's letters, boy. Them's words. Don't tell me you can't read?"

"I'd like to," Gregory said. "Leastways I think I would. I'm Gregory. This here's Maw."

Maw did a loop-de-loop, then dipped her head in a bow.

"Pretty fancy flyin'," the man said. He held out his hand, and Gregory took it. The man backed away. Gregory found himself shaking a hand without a body. The man's real hand popped out of his sleeve. He laughed. "Phineas T. McFlame," he said. "Magic's my game."

That's how Gregory and Maw teamed up with the famous Phineas T., Showman Extraordinaire. Phineas taught Gregory and Maw the ins and outs of the mysterious scratchings as the three of them traveled from Illinois to Missouri and back again, stopping at every backwater crossing and town. Phineas did tricks, and Gregory and Maw performed a little magic of their own.

"Now, Maw," Gregory would say, standing on the steps of the wagon before an assembled crowd. "Got a hankering for a red bonnet today."

Taking her cue, Maw would fly over the crowd, stopping to hover a moment wherever she saw red.

"Nope," Gregory would say. "Not one with a flower.

"Nope. Not a feathered one either, Maw. Today I'm thinking of a red bonnet with a ribbon . . . a blue ribbon. Think you can find it?"

Of course Maw could find it. But first she'd soar so high that the people had to crane their necks and squint just to see her. Then she'd dive straight down at top speed. With a great flapping and cawing, Maw would snatch the bonnet right off the woman's head and take it to Gregory as applause filled the air. Gregory tossed the bonnet back to the lady, who was usually crying tears of happiness at having been part of a real-live magic show. Then Maw would fly through the crowd with a tin cup to collect the coins the people so generously gave.

Gregory and Maw stayed with Phineas for two

years, up until they wowed the citizens of Sharpesville. Remember Sharpesville? Gregory ended the Sharpesville show by asking Maw to find the prettiest girl in town. Maw hardly hesitated. She made a perfect landing on Little Gert's head, presenting the excited child with a pink rose. Little Gert was so thrilled, she ran up and gave Gregory a hug. Beaming with pride, Fiona invited the whole town to her place for a party. One taste of Fiona's huckleberry pie, and Gregory and Maw decided their show days were over.

"We could use a rest," said Gregory.

"I've been itchin' to build a nest," Maw said. "If'n I remember how. Maybe I'll do some courtin'. How'd you like a couple of brothers and sisters?"

Gregory thought that would be just fine.

Sy told about a stretch of bank with good soil just a mile downstream.

Millie offered Gregory all the seeds he and Maw would need for planting a right nice vegetable garden.

"I'll give you a few chickens to get started," Marsh Gibbons said. "You could raise eggs for trade . . . no offense, Maw."

"Thanks just the same," Phineas said when Gregory invited him to stay, too. "But I've got roamin' in my blood, and the show must go on. Hate to see you leave. But it's been fun. Good luck to both you and Maw."

And so they parted. And so Gregory and Maw

built a place of their own along the Pustulli, just a mile downstream from Sharpesville. And that's where we are now. Sharpesville. The day the Mean One rode into town.

When Gregory woke up the morning of the Mean One, he said, "Maw, it's gonna be another scorcher. Better take a couple dozen eggs to town before they hard-boil themselves in the sun. Wanna pack along a few of them peppers Millie favors, too, now that they're ripe."

Gregory fed and watered the chickens and filled a flour sack with eggs. Then he picked four of the largest peppers for Millie. Maw was busy too. Working on her nest. Her nest was coming along fine. It was a work of art. She needed only a few remaining bits and scraps of things before she could start courtin'.

And there they were, bouncing along the road to town — Gregory whistling and Maw crooning her best Crow.

"Life is grand," Gregory said.

"Even on the hottest of days," replied Maw.

"Glad you're my maw," said Gregory.

"Raised you from a babe," said Maw.

"Never to part."

"Love you to pieces."

"What's that smell?" asked Gregory.

Maw's eyes crossed. "Enough to make my feathers molt," she said. "Suppose something died?"

"Weeks ago," Gregory said.

"The heat don't help," said Maw.

"*Mercy*, it stinks!" they blurted together. And they couldn't help but laugh.

They had barely reached the edge of town when they heard the Mean One's shots ring out. Then Little Gert's cry of *Geggie!* Far up the street, beside a billowing curtain of gunsmoke, Gregory saw the townspeople grouped as if sitting for a portrait. Except that no one was smiling.

Maw's eyes could spot a grasshopper from two hundred feet on a fog-filled morning. And she had no trouble making out the man behind the curtain: A giant. With a face ugly enough to stop a train and send it backtracking with its caboose between its legs.

"Hoped I'd never see the day," she said. "Must be that Mean One fella. Thought I smelled a rat."

"A big rat," said Gregory when the smoke finally cleared. "On a horse. And he's looking our way."

4. Justice

What the Mean One saw, squinting down the street toward where the townspeople were looking, was a scarecrow. At least that's what he thought he saw. For though Gregory had a soul that could outshine the moon, he had never been much for looks.

"Thin as a bean and bony as a rabbit's foot . . . God love the boy," Maw often said fondly of Gregory.

It was true. Gregory had a hard time filling out his clothes. In a strong wind, the air went rushing up his trousers, blew past his waist, and made a sail of his shirt before whistling out his wrists. If he pinched and loosened the cuff of his sleeve just right, he could lay down a tune as good as any jug band this side of Memphis.

The Mean One was sure the townspeople had stuck the scarecrow there to frighten him off. And he laughed at what fools they must be.

"Why, that heap of sticks and rags couldn't scare a — " He stopped, the split ends of his beard bristling as he squinted harder. "A bird!" he finished. "A crow! It's got a crow sittin' right on its shoulder."

"A dead crow," he added, stretching out an arm and taking aim.

"NO!" chorused Fiona and the others.

But the Mean One wasn't about to let slip an opportunity for target practice. His finger pulled through the trigger as easily as a bear's tooth slicing through a honeycomb. There was a click as the gun's hammer fell.

"Shucks," he said. "Used up all my bullets on my entrance." He was about to reload when a squeaky voice rose from the crowd. The voice belonged to Victoria Odabee, who was something of a celebrity in town, having once taken fifth place in the Harrison County baton-twirling contest.

"Please, Your Meanness," Victoria squeaked. "Wouldn't you rather dazzle us with your gun twirling? I've heard so much about it. I'd love to see a real professional go at it."

The Mean One winced and spat out a hunk of green and yellow phlegm at the word *love*. But his chest puffed out at the compliment, nonetheless.

"Yeah. You're right. I've got all day to splatter that crow." And he blew a sour breath across the barrel of each gun, then sent the guns spinning around his fingers until they were blurs of silver light.

Though their hearts were still in their throats over Maw's brush with death, the townsfolk were mightily impressed. Especially Victoria. Victoria's eyes slid back and forth in their sockets, attempting to focus on first one, then the other of the whirling barrels.

The Mean One could see he had the crowd right where he wanted them. Quick as a blink, he stopped the guns' forward spinning, reversing the motion with a backward flick of the wrists. It was a cruel move. You could almost hear the eyes of the townspeople crashing gears. Marsh Gibbons thought he'd gone blind. His pupils were jammed up under his eyelids like a couple of corn kernels stuck between molars.

Marsh swatted his forehead with the heel of his hand. His eyeballs were jolted free. "I can see! I can see!" he cried.

The preacher was overcome with emotion. Forgetting that Marsh had never been blind at all, he yelled, "Praise God! A miracle!"

The Mean One's chest puffed out even further. "Call it what ya like," he said. And with a final flourish of spinning, he slapped the guns into their holsters, a twin smacking of leather slicing the air.

It was then that the Mean One's horse let go with an ungodly whinny. The brute swept his head from side to side and thumped the ground angrily with both forelegs.

"Easy, Killer," the Mean One said.

But the horse would not be eased. He bared his teeth, a trainlike growl coming from deep within his throat.

"Another? So soon?" said the Mean One. "But you chased one all morning. You gotta watch yourself in this heat."

Killer snorted and thumped the ground again. Actually, it was more of a bam than a thump, as if he were trying to smash the daylights out of something unseen there on the street.

The Mean One grinned. "One-track mind, eh?" He leaned forward in his saddle, studying the faces of those cowering before him. "Seems my horse wants a sheriff to play with," he said. "Which one of you yokels is the law in this town?"

Poor Amos Fletcher nearly swallowed his Adam's apple at this. The man went into a dead faint, tumbling out of his chair, limp as a rag doll. Sy caught him just as he was about to bop his head on the boardwalk. Millie dropped to her knees, fanning Amos with one hand while reaching into the bosom of her dress for her smelling salts with the other.

"We got no sheriff," Millie said, her voice bumpy

with dread. "Never did." She looked wild-eyed at the others for support.

The people weren't about to surrender Amos — unconscious or not — to the likes of Killer, who by this time had bashed himself a good-sized hole in the earth and was working on a second.

"Nope," someone said.

"No sheriff here."

"Never seen one."

"What's a sheriff?"

"Hot enough for y'all?" chimed Gregory, who arrived just then with Maw riding his shoulder. Worried for their friends, the two had made their way up the street during the hubbub of the gun twirling and subsequent miracle. Gregory was so glad to see everyone that his happiness came pouring out in a flood of excited chatter.

"Gawd, it's a real stink-out! What gives? Kinda hard to breathe, ain't it? Got a sack full of eggs to trade. Prob'ly cooked by now. And some of them peppers. What do you call them, Millie?"

"Hot chilis," Millie replied softly, still ministering to Amos. She looked up for an instant, smiling sadly, thinking it might be the last time she and Gregory would see each other.

Having worked the top off her vial of smelling salts, Millie now waved the salts under Amos' nose. Amos stirred, groaning, his eyes blinking open. One look at the Mean One made him realize he'd be better off asleep. His hand rose slightly in a wave. "Night-night," he murmured before checking out again.

"What happened to Sheriff Fletcher?" Gregory asked.

Sy shook his head — so strongly that his new, made-in-Paris toupee slid dangerously to one side. "Who . . . Periff?" he rushed to say. "Periff Sheffer? . . . No, old Periff's all right. Heat's got him a little low is all."

Both Gregory and Maw thought the heat wasn't being all that kind to Sy either. That, or Sy's dentures were giving him trouble again. Then Maw reminded Gregory of his manners, and Gregory turned to the stranger who towered above the scene, still fannied to his saddle.

"I'm Gregory," Gregory said. "This is Maw. Pleasure to meet you."

"Why, look, Killer," the Mean One said. "It ain't a scarecrow at all. It's a boy. Crow's real, though. Never saw such a mangy-looking creature. Glad I saved my ammo."

Maw let the insult slide. Those struck by love usually have little to say. They just stare at the object of their desire. Which is what Maw was doing. Staring at the Mean One's beard.

"It's perfect," she bobbed to Gregory after shaking off the spell. "Look at that bush! Why, a beakful of that would make my nest. I could weave those stiff bristles through the whole affair. Wouldn't even have to add mud, by the looks of it. Think of the strength it would provide. The beauty. Matches my color scheme, too."

"Now, Maw," Gregory said. "That's the man's own hair. Maybe if he decides to shave or let Sy give him a trim, he'd be nice enough to offer you some. But you can't just fly over and grab yourself a patch without being invited."

Maw sighed, still studying the matted mass that was the Mean One's beard. She calculated it wouldn't take but an hour or two to pick out the old fish bones and dried beads of catsup stuck throughout.

The Mean One didn't like being stared at googly-eyed by a crow. Especially by a crow he thought he should have splattered with gunshot some time before.

With a movement so quick and fluid that it belied his hugeness, the Mean One grabbed Maw around the middle, pinning her wings and whisking her off Gregory's shoulder. He lifted her up with a triumphant grunt, holding her high above his head.

Maw kicked her little legs feverishly. She tried pecking her way to freedom. But the Mean One only laughed. "That tickles," he said before propping his topmost finger under her beak so that she looked like a soldier suddenly coming to attention. "I hate being tickled."

Gregory went crazy with anger and fear for Maw. He lunged, pounding his fists against the

Mean One's leg. "You stop that! That's my maw. How dare you!"

Such courage inspired the townspeople. They hissed their disapproval. Some clicked their tongues. Fiona's tongue was put to better use. "You beast!" she hollered. "Unhand that poor defense-less crow."

Little Gert had been watching everything through her knothole. It made her powerful mad to see Maw being treated so. "Big bully," Gertie told the oak staves of her barrel. Then she rocked her-self back and forth, causing the barrel to sway, until it overbalanced to one side and crashed to the ground. Freed at last, Little Gert ran past a horrified Fiona and straight for the Mean One, yell-ing, "Bad man . . . bad man."

"Baby!" Fiona screamed. "You'll be killed!"

Sensing there was some fun to be had in all this, the Mean One swiped Gregory aside and dug his spurs into Killer. The horse reared with an awful sound and took off like a shot.

Maw's legs swung out behind the Mean One's hand with the sudden rush of air. Gregory revved his skinny legs and charged after horse and rider. "Hold on, Maw . . . I'm coming!"

"Me too!" cried Gertie.

Fiona went hysterical. "My pride, my joy, my dumplin'!" she spluttered, lifting her mass of skirts and huffing after Gert.

Worried for Fiona's health, Millie dropped

Amos's head. "Your blood pressure!" she called, rushing for Fiona with smelling salts at the ready.

Amos's head smacked the boardwalk, jarring him awake. He watched the stars circle behind his eyes. "Ain't no sheriff," he mumbled. "Never — "

"Shut up, Amos," Marsh said. "Can't you see Maw's in a dung heap of trouble?" He helped Amos find his feet, and the two hit the chase. Sy followed, a hand clamped to his toupee. Victoria came next, squeaking at the top of her lungs. Soon the whole town was up and running in a line after the Mean One, who charged up one side of Main Street and down the other, laughing and yelling *EEEE-AAAHHHH!* with Maw's feet tracing circles in the air.

The pursuit continued with a blizzard of dust in its wake. Up. Down. All around the town. Until the Mean One — with an evil grin — used his enormous weight to pull up sharply on the reins, stopping Killer in his tracks.

Gregory plowed straight into Killer, bouncing off the mammoth horse like a moth ricocheting off a lamp-lit window. An instant later, Little Gert smashed into Gregory.

"Watch out!" "Oh, no!" "Ouch!" came a flurry of shouts as one by one the townsfolk crashed and tumbled into one another like a line of human dominoes.

"You put Maw down, or else," Gregory yelled, using his skinniness to pull free from the mass of arms and legs.

"Okay," said the Mean One. "I'll put her down." And he did. He released his grip, and Maw fell a full eight feet to the ground.

"I'll take you instead," the Mean One spat, grabbing a fistful of Gregory's collar. He would have lifted Gregory off the ground and started another chase, except that there was so little of Gregory inside the shirt that the boy was able to squiggle free, leaving the Mean One with only a surprised look and a handful of rumpled shirt.

Gregory quickly scooped up Maw and somersaulted beyond the monster's reach. The others had disentangled themselves by this time, and they moved back too — watching, waiting, expecting the worst.

"That was mean and nasty and rude, what you did to Maw," Gregory shouted as he cradled his dazed mother. "Maw, you all right? Maw? Speak to me!"

"Ca-awwww," Maw managed weakly. She kept shaking herself as if to throw off the weight of the hand she still felt squeezed to her middle. Her heart was drumming triple time. Gregory crooked his finger and ran it gently past Maw's head and down her back, smoothing her ruffled feathers. "Don't die, Maw. Don't."

Maw's body stiffened. Gregory feared it was the end.

"Not by a long shot!" Maw suddenly exclaimed. "Ain't no one gonna lay this body to rest till I teach that lummox a lesson." She spoke in Crow, which was just as well, for her feelings were vented in such a rush of unsavory terms that Gregory's ears burned scarlet.

"Now, Maw," Gregory said when Maw added a new threat to her tongue-lashing. "I don't think that'd be such a good idea."

"He deserves as much and more," Maw said angrily. And she shot out of Gregory's hands like a comet, winging her way high up. For a moment she thought she was back with Phineas T. again, performing. Except that this performance would be different. With a raucous shriek, she started her dive. She was a flash of blackness. A hurtling piece of wonder. A streaking . . . Well, she was fast.

"This time I'll pull that scrawny neck right off its hinges," the Mean One boasted, dropping Gregory's shirt and raising his fist. He had to crane his head so far back that his oversized hat fell clean off.

It was something to see, the way Maw pulled out of her dive just ten feet above the Mean One's head. For a second she hovered there, setting her sights. Then she let loose. She did. Some might call it crude. Some might call it dirty.

"*Justice*" is what Maw called out as a swatch of white fell with perfect accuracy, landing with a splat in the center of the Mean One's upturned forehead.

5. Tears?

Now there's something that needs to be said here about human nature. And it's this. Doesn't matter where or when it takes place, but if a bird's bodily release suddenly plops down from tree or sky and lands on a person's head and others see what has happened — the result is the same.

First, there's shock. Those who witness the event stare in disbelief. "Is that what I think it is?" they say to themselves. "Can't be."

After the initial shock comes a smile. A teeny smile. Just a hint of a smile. But as the scene replays itself in your mind, the hint of smile grows larger. You begin to shake your head. You can't believe it. It's so . . . so . . . well, it's funny. *Really* funny. And before you know it, you're laughing. Not just a teeny laugh. But a laugh that starts deep down in your belly and rumbles forth to shake your everything. And that's exactly how it was for Gregory and Sy and Fiona and Marsh and the others. Even Maw, bless her revenged little heart.

Suddenly great guffaws of laughter exploded from the crowd. Fingers were pointed. Some folks dropped to the ground, holding their sides, eyes wet with the perfect hilarity and rightness of it all.

Too stunned to even hear the laughter at first, the Mean One lifted a hand, his fingers touching the liquidy mass that was making its way through the unkempt hairs of his brows. He flinched, his tongue shooting past his lips as if he'd just swallowed a cupful of snake oil. Pulling a grubby handkerchief from his vest, he wiped the degradation from both head and fingers before releasing the handkerchief as one drops a dead mouse onto the backyard compost.

Only then did the laughter reach him, his chest, shoulders, and face swelling with the ridicule so that it looked to Gregory as if the man's anger might burst clear through his eyeholes.

But it wasn't anger that burst through the glassy hardness of those popped orbs. For just then in each of the Mean One's eyes there suddenly appeared a tiny sphere . . . a little round of clearness about the size of a baby pearl. The pearls grew ever so slowly, becoming rounder and fuller, until they dropped from their own weight, sliding past the man's pitted cheeks before being swabbed by the forest of his beard.

There were gasps as the townsfolk cut off their laughter in mid breath. Those few who continued to titter now pulled back their pointing fingers.

"Tears?" someone whispered.

The word floated delicate as a soap bubble through the still air.

"Tears?"

"Tears?"

"Cherish the day."

Gregory was just as surprised as the others. He whirled toward Maw.

"Ain't my fault the maniac tried to kill me," Maw said. "He deserved it."

"I think he's hurtin'," Gregory replied.

Maw turned away, scratching the earth with one foot as though searching for something. "If'n he can cry, I guess he can't be all bad," she said stiffly. Looking up again, she caught Gregory's thin smile.

"Well, don't just stand there gawking," she blurted. "Go see if the brute needs some help." She folded back her wings with a *humph*. "But don't expect me to apologize. 'Cause I won't!"

Gregory threw on his shirt. "You're a hard one," he said, his voice colored proud.

Course it wasn't Maw's justice — embarrassing though it was — that had brought tears to the

Mean One's eyes. It was the townspeople's laughter. For the laughter had triggered a recollection in the giant's dust-filled brain. A recollection from his past . . . so dim he couldn't make out what it was. It was like he'd been pricked by a pin. A pinprick of sadness. But a pinprick doesn't last long.

Gregory had taken only two steps toward the slumping giant when the Mean One snapped upright again in his saddle. Drawing the back of his hand across his face, the man was surprised to find some wet there. "What?" he boomed. "Y'all laughing at me? Why, I'll flatten every last one of ya . . . make sawdust out of this town!"

His stare found Maw. "But first I'm gonna enjoy picking out this one's feathers one at a time. . . . Slow and painful." He cuffed the handles of his guns. "I'll make Swiss cheese out of whatever's left."

Maw took a sudden aversion to Swiss cheese. The Mean One dismounted with a grunt, smacking the ground like a felled tree.

Glad to be free of such a weight, Killer snorted, licking away the ring of foam that had formed around his mouth. The horse must have spotted Amos' badge during the chase, because he suddenly bolted for the livery stables. It took him only a moment to snoot out the silver star lying in the street. With a trumpeting whicker, he reared, then proceeded to give the badge a proper burial.

The Mean One reloaded his guns in case there

was anything left of Maw after the plucking. He reloaded slowly, enjoying the silent shivers of the townsfolk as each bullet slid into its chamber.

"It's what I get for procrastinatin'," Maw said. "Should've made out my will long before this. Everything I own is yours," she told Gregory. "Ain't much, but it's all yours. I'll miss the dickens out of you. Maybe we can meet up again in the hereafter."

The townsfolk were inching their way back toward the boardwalk. "I'll shoot the next thing that moves!" the Mean One said, causing everyone's leg muscles to stop right where they were.

Sy stopped along with everyone else. The sudden halt prompted his toupee to slink to one side again, and he twisted his mouth and blew upward in an attempt to keep the hairpiece from sliding any farther. The toupee slipped another inch in spite of his efforts.

"It moved!" bellowed the Mean One, charging and grabbing the hair. With a flick of his wrist, the toupee sprang into the air, sailing floppy, like some unlucky squirrel shot from a cannon. Quickly, the Mean One aimed and fired. The townsfolk winced at the collision of lead and fur. Sy whimpered as he watched his made-in-Paris hair float down all along Main Street, one strand at a time.

"I can't believe you done that!" Gregory told the Mean One. "Next to how you treated Maw, that's the meanest thing I ever saw. How can you be so mean?"

"Practice," the Mean One spat. "I've always been mean."

"But surely not always?" Gregory said, truly curious. "You couldn't have been born mean?"

The Mean One grinned, baring the holes where a couple of teeth were missing. "Yep."

"But that's impossible," said Maw.

"Is it?" the Mean One said with a leer. Lashing out, he palmed Gregory's head as though calculating the ripeness of a small melon. The townspeople's mouths sprang open to voice their concern. Maw clapped her wings, prepared to do her duty again if the occasion called for it. But, surprisingly, the Mean One only pressed Gregory's head to his massive chest. "What do you hear?" he asked.

Gregory squinted as he listened. The stench was dizzying. "Nothing," he said. "I don't hear a thing."

"See? I don't have a heart."

"Nonsense," said Maw. "Everybody's got a heart."

"I DON'T!" the Mean One blared. With his free hand he dug a finger into his ear, giving the oversized digit a turn, becoming suddenly reflective. "Don't believe I ever had one. Else I lost it somewhere along the way."

Struggling for air and speaking into the Mean One's greasy leather vest, Gregory said, "But — "

"But what?" said the Mean One, pulling back his arm so that Gregory had sole possession of his head again.

Gregory didn't *know* what . . . other than he was glad to have his head freed.

Maw tried steering the Mean One's thoughts away from feather picking and Swiss cheese. "What the boy means is that it's only natural for a man to have a heart."

"Right," said Gregory. "Why, a man without a heart is like . . . like . . . like a snake without a tongue or a toad without warts or . . ."

"A skunk without its smell," Maw added, forcing air through her nostrils and wishing the Mean One weren't standing upwind of what little breeze there was.

"I got all three," the Mean One boasted. And just to prove it, he stuck out his tongue while pointing to a trio of warts on his neck, elbow raised so that the townsfolk got a heady whiff of his crusted armpit.

"Then it's only a heart you be lacking," Gregory said. "And maybe . . . maybe . . ." He allowed a moment for the idea to take root. "Maybe Maw and I could help you find it."

"We *could*?" said Maw. "I mean, we could!" she quickly added. "Boy's right."

"Yeah," came murmurs of agreement from the crowd.

"Boy's right."

"Find his heart."

"Good idea."

"Darn tootin'."

The Mean One furrowed his brow. "How's come I need a heart, anyway?" he said.

"A person has to have a ticker," Gregory said. "Everyone knows that."

The Mean One scratched his whiskers, releasing a snowfall of dander that settled like a sheen of ash on his boots. "I don't even know where I lost my heart . . . if I ever had one in the first place."

"I'm good at finding things, aren't I, Mama?" Little Gert piped.

"You stay out of this," Fiona put in quickly. "Finding hearts is not child's play."

Sy nodded his now-naked head. "A lost heart is a heart lost," he said wisely. "Same as a head of hair. What's gone is gone. What's found is found. . . ." He twirled the one strand of hair he'd managed to pluck from the air, his expression turning confused. "Or something like that."

The Mean One took a fistful of tobacco from his shirt pocket and shoved it into his mouth. He rolled the tobacco around, chewing some, then tongued the mass against a cheek, the sound of spurting saliva and squishing tobacco clearly audible. Suddenly he spat out a line of brown juice, the juice hitting the dirt in front of Gregory and Maw. Gregory felt some spray patter his bare toes. Maw's ankles twitched with the same sensation. Together they took a step back as two stunned ants struggled out of the circle of sludge at their feet.

"Okay," the Mean One said. "I'll make you a deal. You find my heart, you live — maybe. You don't find it, you die. Most likely you'll die either way. Twenty-four hours. That's all the time you got."

Gregory would have liked better terms, but knew not to press his luck. He looked to Maw, who had always told him there wasn't anything they couldn't do if they put their minds to it. "What do you say, Maw?"

Maw thought the idea of staying alive another twenty-four hours was a good one. But as for finding the Mean One's heart — "I don't know. Looks to me like we'd have to go back in time. If'n he lost his heart, it must have been in the past." She shrugged. "Never been anywhere but the present myself. Don't know anyone who has."

"Guess it'll be a challenge then," Gregory said, knowing how a challenge was second only to worms on Maw's list of favored things.

"Never yet run from a good challenge," Maw answered, squaring her shoulders. "We'll do it!"

The townsfolk were relieved to know Sharpesville wouldn't be turned to sawdust just then. At once Fiona thought about finishing up that huckleberry pie she'd left in the icebox. She figured she had enough berries left to bake two additional pies, and she'd get them eaten, too, before the twenty-four hours wore out.

Gregory put out his hand to the Mean One so they could shake on it. The Mean One ignored the offer. Instead, he spat a fresh gob of tobacco juice upward, hitting the weather vane atop Millie's store. The metal rooster spun with a pinging sound. Satisfied with his aim, the Mean One wiped away the drool that had stayed behind on his chin.

"Twenty-four hours," he said. "Startin' now."

And that was how Gregory and Maw agreed to take the Mean One back through time.

6. The Plan

On second thought, Maw said she wasn't going anywhere till the Mean One took an oath. "He needs to promise to behave like a decent human animal," she told Gregory. "Can't be taking someone that big into the past if I got to be all the time looking over my shoulder and fearing the worst."

Gregory agreed and called for the preacher.

"If it ain't too much trouble," he told the Mean One, "Maw and I would feel better if you swore an oath first."

"Oh, I'm good at swearing!" the Mean One said. He had a hand over the place on his chest where his heart should have been. "It hurts," he said.

"Not having a heart hurts. Always thought it was indigestion."

Gregory stood to one side of the giant, and Maw took the other. The preacher proffered his Bible. "Raise your right hand and repeat after me," he said.

The Mean One put out both hands. There was enough topsoil wedged up under his nails to start a fair-sized kitchen garden.

"That one," Gregory said, tapping the right hand by way of a hint.

"Knew it all along," said the Mean One. "Just testing ya."

The preacher stretched himself tall. "Now, then, do you solemnly swear to behave yourself for the duration of this trip? From this hour forward. For better or worse. In sickness and in health. Whether in the present or past. And whatever else I may have left out — so help you God?"

An irreverent smile snaked across the Mean One's face. Suddenly he let loose with every cuss word Gregory had ever heard . . . as well as a goodly many the boy's ears had never before had the misfortune of taking in.

"How's that?" the Mean One asked when he'd run out of breath.

Visibly shaken, the preacher used a hand to help his jaw back into position. "Y-you're supposed to say *I do*," he said.

"I do *what*?" barked the Mean One.

"I do *swear*," said the preacher.

"Heck, didn't ya hear me? If you want, I can give it another go." He was about to repeat his litany of cuss words when the preacher said, "NO! Please!"

"It's a promise you'll be making," Gregory tried explaining. "That you'll act decent while we look for your heart."

The Mean One stared vacant as a swimming hole in the middle of winter. Maw figured the words *promise* and *decent* weren't likely in his vocabulary. She took a different tack. "Who-all here wants to make sawdust of this town?" she asked.

"I DO!" shouted the Mean One.

As Maw nodded her satisfaction, a most radiant smile lit up the preacher's face. He cocked his head as though catching the strains of harps playing nearby. His honeyed gaze steadied on the Mean One before dropping to Maw.

"Then through the power invested in me," he said, "I now pronounce you man and — "

Luckily, he never finished. Maw's outcry caused him to chomp into his tongue instead. She let out a squawk of such magnitude that Thelma Wingate — who was pushing ninety and all but deaf — suddenly found herself doing the dog paddle three feet above her rocker. "Lord, take thy servant home," Thelma cried, thinking it was Judgment Day.

"Kinda got your ceremonies mixed up, didn't

you, Reverend?" Marsh said when Thelma had landed safely, catching her rocker on the back-swing.

The preacher spoke carefully around his in-jured tongue. "Thorry," he said. "Forth of habit. My mithtake."

"I'll say!" Maw croaked as she gasped to refill her lungs. Having come within an eyelash of being hitched to a most malodorous husband, she leaned against the boardwalk with one wing while fanning herself with the other.

As for the Mean One, Maw's blast had struck the heartless hollow of his chest square on. The emptiness acted like a drum, so that even now one thunderous echo after another was sent coursing through his body. With each aftershock he shud-dered and shook, twitched and pitched, rumba'd and samba'd . . . until gravity won out, the echoes finding their way to his feet. From there they exited through his boots to be absorbed into the ground with burpy tremors.

"Lightning!" the Mean One said. "I been hit." And he glared at the cloudless sky before falling back onto the walk, exhausted.

With the oath administered and a terrible mis-take averted, Maw roused herself and got down to the business at hand. "It's one thing to want to go back in time," she said. "It's another to actually do it." She scampered out a ways into the street and began pacing. "Anybody got any ideas?"

The townsfolk crinkled their faces. All except

Gregory, who fell into step behind Maw. "There has to be a way," he said. "Let's everyone think."

At once the air sizzled hotter with the straining of so many brains. Eyes vibrated. Toes flexed. Ears wiggled. Heads and tummies were scratched. Some looked skyward for inspiration. Others doodled in the street or fingered sums in the air.

The Mean One thought too. Though he wasn't much used to it. "Time, back . . . back, time," he mumbled in his cavernous voice. But all he got for his efforts was a headache and a stirring in his stomach.

"I'm hungry!" he said. "Thinkin' makes me hungry."

Fiona cringed. She knew all too well what hunger could do to a person. Once Thelma's dog, Bullet, had helped herself to two fresh pies that Fiona had put on the windowsill to cool. Fiona had been fasting all day in order to plunge guilt free into the pies come suppertime. When she found Bullet licking up the last of the pies, she'd gone into a fit, flinging pots and pans and whatever else she could reach after the berry-faced hound. Fiona hated to think what a hungry Mean One might do.

"Gregory's got the best-tasting eggs in town," she said, pointing to Gregory's sack. "I'm sure he wouldn't mind if you helped yourself to a few."

The Mean One grunted. He plunged a hand into the sack and drew out an egg. Sniffing once, he popped the egg into his mouth, shell and all.

"I've got it!" Amos suddenly cried through the

Mean One's crunchings. "Hap Pearson said he saw his whole life flash before his eyes. You remember Hap. Fell a good sixty feet when we was puttin' the new roof on the church. Hap went back in time, all right. Said he could remember everything, even back to when he was a baby."

"Didn't old Hap die from that fall?" Marsh asked.

Amos sucked his teeth. "Now that you mention it, he did. But he died happy, true to his name, cooing in my arms like the babe he'd become."

"You fixin' on pushing me off a *roof*?" the Mean One said, egg goo slipping out the corners of his mouth. He was already on his fourth egg and showed no signs of stopping.

Amos went ashen. He saw his own life flash before his eyes. "Mom always said I got the dumbest ideas," he stammered. "Don't I, everyone? Don't I get the dumbest ideas?"

"Dumb," everyone concurred.

Sy had been quietly fishing the waters of his mind, and he jumped up then, having caught a whopper.

"Hypnotism!" he said. "That's the ticket. Seen it done once myself."

He quickly pulled a gold watch from his fob pocket and held it up by its chain. "All you do is look hard while I swing it," he told Millie.

Millie's eyes swerved back and forth to follow the swinging watch.

"Sleepy," said Sy. "You're getting sleepy. Sleepier . . . so sleepy . . . sl — "

"Sy!" Millie yelled. "Sy, confound it, wake up!" She gave him a bop on the head, and Sy's eyelids fluttered open.

"It worked!" he said. "I dreamed I owned a barbershop in Jeff City, and the gov'nor himself came in for a shave."

"You've never even been to Jeff City," Millie said.

Sy knew it was true. "I must have traveled to the future," he said. "Sorry." But he was secretly pleased to know he'd make it big in the capital one day.

Gregory had stopped his pacing to watch Sy's demonstration. "I'm afraid hypnotism won't work," he said. "Either will dyin'," he told Amos. "What we need is a vehicle. Something to take me and Maw and the Mean One back through time and home again in one piece."

"I once heard about a machine that travels through time," Marsh said. "All you do is hop in, set the thingamajigs, and off you go."

Millie shook her head. "I'd have to special order the thingamajigs," she said. "That could take weeks."

Maw had been scratching figures and symbols in the street for some time now. She had a storm of numbers laid out at her feet. There were pictures too — stacks of things that looked like boxes, and a creature of some kind.

"What you got there, Maw?" Gregory asked.

"Much simpler than I ever thought it could be," Maw said. "Answer me this: How much wood could a woodchuck chuck if a woodchuck could chuck wood?"

"Beats me," Gregory said. "I suppose it depends on how fast he was chucking."

"Bingo!" said Maw. "That's exactly what I came up with. Speed! It all boils down to speed. You can't just mosey on into the past. You've got to explode into it . . . take it by surprise."

"Shoo! Scat! Shoo!" Fiona hollered just then, breaking Gregory's concentration. She was waving her arms toward the church, which stood blazing in a fresh coat of whitewash at the end of the street. She was yelling at Killer, who had stretched himself out in the bed of zinnias she and Millie had only recently planted for the upcoming church bazaar.

Killer gave no indication that he heard Fiona's shouts. The horse merely moved onto his side and began rolling in the flowers as if relieving an itch.

"The nerve!" Fiona said. She thrust both little fingers under her tongue and blew. It was more air than whistle that came out.

The Mean One swallowed the last of Gregory's eggs (he'd eaten all twenty-four) and belched loudly. "I wouldn't do that if I was you," he said.

Fiona was too worked up to pay him any mind. She rearranged her pinkies and blew again, this time harder.

Some say the horse started running even before he'd stood. Most recount hearing thunder and seeing a brown blur akin to a tumbleweed in a twister. Fiona moved pretty quick herself, diving straight for Sy's arms. Sy might have caught her too, if his hands hadn't been at his sides. The two hit the ground just as Killer streaked to a halt at the exact spot from which Fiona had whistled. The horse swung his muzzle over the spot, sniffing and snorting and slobbering.

"Killer's hungry," the Mean One said. "I always whistle like that when it's feeding time."

"Maw!" Gregory cried. "Did you get an eyeful of that horse?"

Maw checked her figures. "Might be fast enough," she said. "But does he go backward? We aim to go back in time, not forward."

"Oh, Killer'll go backward, all right," the Mean One said. "If he don't like what's in front of him."

"Like what?" Gregory asked. "What doesn't he like?"

"Yapping," answered the Mean One. "And howling. He hates hound dogs for just that reason. They hurt his ears."

Everyone knew Thelma's dog, Bullet, was the town's loudest yapper. Everyone, of course, except Thelma. Being deaf, Thelma thought Bullet was as mute as a picture on the wall. Gregory was at the old woman's rocker before you could count to three.

"No need to shout," Thelma said. "I can read lips, you know. Sure, you can borrow Bullet. Though she ain't much of a watchdog. Poor thing tries hard enough. Has her mouth open most day and night. But nothin' ever comes out."

It was Amos who volunteered to run to Thelma's for Bullet, grateful to put some distance between himself and Killer, who had begun sniffing in the sheriff's direction.

"Keep her leashed," Maw called after him. "Stop at the church and wait for our signal." She nodded to Gregory, and the two stepped aside to confer, Maw moving her wings like a pint-sized bandleader and Gregory bobbing his replies in Crow.

"What about my heart?" the Mean One growled from the boardwalk. Oath or no oath, he felt like hitting something, and he pulled himself up to see who was available. Suddenly the ground moved beneath him. He clutched his belly, overcome by a real case of indigestion at having eaten so many eggs so fast. His knees buckled and his face turned a froggy shade of green. With a thud, he fell back to the walk.

Gregory and Maw ended their powwow and ran to where the Mean One sat groaning. "We'll need some particulars," Maw said.

"Like when and where were you born?" Gregory added.

"That's easy," the Mean One said, pulling the shirt down over his right shoulder. "Had it tattooed right here so's I wouldn't forget."

Gregory leaned close to read the blue-black ink pricked into the man's hairy shoulder. "April first, 1881," he said.

"Where?" asked Maw.

The Mean One skinned his shirt over the other shoulder. "Got that, too. What's it say? I don't read too good."

"Flat Rock," Gregory replied.

"That's a hundred miles due south," Marsh said. "Not much there but scrubland and jack-rabbits."

"A ghost town, ain't it?" asked Sy.

"It is now," the Mean One said. "Me and Killer leveled the place a good while back." His health seemed to improve at the mention of it. "Had to. Hated that town. Bad memories. Though I can't recollect 'em now."

Having learned the magic of numbers from Phineas T., Maw went to work, scraping a smooth place in the dirt in front of her. She used her toe to scratch in a 4 — "for April being the fourth month," she said. Then she added a 1 for the day of the Mean One's birth . . . and a 1-8-8-1 for the year. She put plus signs between them all.

"Four plus one plus one plus eight plus eight plus one," she said. "What do you get, son?"

"Twenty-three!" Gregory shouted.

"Yep. And two plus three is five." She turned to Sy. "Think you can lend us that watch of yours? We'll set it for five, so's we'll be sure to end up where we're going."

Sy was proud to be of assistance. He pulled out his watch, the dial emblazoned with a tiny locomotive, and handed it to Gregory. "Wind it whenever you like," he said. "Doesn't run anyway."

"Don't need nothin' fancy," Maw replied as Gregory set the hour to five. "Killer will be doing all the running we require — which reminds me, that horse'll need some fuel."

"That's one thing I don't have to special order," Millie said, racing for her shop. She returned to find the townsfolk mumbling excitedly as they lined up in the center of the street facing Killer, whose backside had been turned to point south. The Mean One sat tall in the saddle. He looked as mean as ever, his stomach on the mend, his face back to its former color.

In front of the giant sat Gregory, eyes flashing with anticipation. Perched on Gregory's shoulder was Maw — a feathery lookout for the strange four-legged ship that was about to make history.

Millie burst through the crowd and handed the bulging oat bag to Gregory. "This should be enough to get you to the past and back," she said.

Gregory felt Maw's claws pinch into his skin. "We leave something out, Maw?"

"Just worried a touch," said Maw. "Not sure this horse will be up to the kind of speed we need."

Gregory wrinkled his brow. The idea came all at once, fully formed, stinging his brain like the crack of a bullwhip. "No need to fret," he told Maw.

"Got a little insurance right here in my pocket."

There was a *yap-yowl-yip-yip* then as Bullet came charging into view up by the church. Amos appeared a second later, heels digging for traction, arms stretched taut by the pull of the leash. "Dad-burned hound!" He wrenched harder, the big dog skittering back on her haunches and howling in frustration. Killer's ears stiffened at the sound, but relaxed some when he saw how the dog stayed put.

"Hurry!" Maw yelled.

Gregory's pulse quickened. He reached for the hot chilis in his pocket and grabbed two. His eyes watered from the heat as he shredded both peppers into the oat bag.

"Ready!" he said.

"Don't forget to write," Victoria squeaked.

"Stand back!" Maw shouted to the crowd. "If'n he backfires, it could turn nasty."

Gregory gripped the saddle horn with one hand and swung the bag over Killer's head with the other.

"Look, Killer . . . food!"

The horse plunged his muzzle into the oats, snorting his gratitude and gobbling one mouthful after another. From her lookout position on Gregory's shoulder, Maw crowed for Amos to release Bullet.

Bullet bounded toward the crowd as if sprung from a trap. Killer heard the high-pitched bugling at the same time he felt the peppers' heat take hold of his mouth. He let go with some music of his own as he tried to shake the fire from his tonsils.

"Hang on, Maw!" Gregory cried, closing his eyes.

"*Ah-ooooooo!*" blared Bullet.

"*Ah-eeeeeee!*" answered Killer, eyes bulging as the pepper fire reached his belly. The horse jumped straight up, legs churning, then came back down and recaught the ground. With his tail pronged to point the way and his tongue hanging behind like a rudder, he shot into motion.

The townsfolk watched in awe as, in a flash, both horse and riders were gone. Flat out, slap-bang, in a tick GONE. Leaving only a tunnel of stirred-up dust in their wake. The people rubbernecked it to the south. And there, already far out on the edge of town, was something that resembled the spinning curtain of a dust devil . . . skimming, skittering, whirling.

There was a sound, too. A wild, raucous, happy sound hanging fat in the air as if it could in no way keep up with its makers. Even Thelma heard it. And jumping up from her rocker with new-found rejuvenation, she threw back her head and let loose, echoing what her ears reported.

"*EEEE-AHHH,*" she cried. "Ride 'im cowboy!"

7. S.A.D. Undertaking

And what a ride it was. Killer went from *Fast* to *FASTer* to *FASTEST!* in three shakes of a squirrel's tail. He backpedaled into the past with his tail sniffing like a divining rod. He had one thing on his mind: *Water. Find water.*

The "Ride 'im cowboy" that Gregory, Maw, and the Mean One had hollered on takeoff was replaced by cries of *Moly! Cawsome!* and *Whoaaa!* as the ground, hills, trees, and sky became dizzying flickers of light and dark, light and dark. . . . Until all three riders were sure it was the scenery that was moving and they who were standing still.

To beat all, Sy's watch started running again. Maw caught a glimpse of it when she pulled her neck into her shoulders to keep her head from being ripped off by the rushing air. The watch stuck straight out in the current, threatening to pull free of its chain, whose links were making a deep impression on the back of Gregory's neck. Maw saw the watch's hands chasing each other like a cat charging after its own tail — the locomotive on the dial spewing steam as if it were the real thing.

Traveling at such a speed does something to a body. Mostly it tickles. So that you can't help laughing. Those who pay attention to history have long wondered about the mysterious laughing whirlwind that shot through a hundred-mile stretch of Pustulli River country between the years 1881 and 1906.

STRANGEST OCCURRENCE EVER, the newspapers of those bygone years report. METEORITE WHOOPS THROUGH TOWN. CACKLING NEW LIFE FORM SPOTTED. GIGGLING TWISTER SAID TO BE NO JOKE! the headlines blare.

From Hokum to Hooterville. Hickory Valley to Hackleburg.

Horses spooked.

Children distracted from their studies.

Hundreds of cases of whiplash reported as necks swiveled to follow the streaking something trailing jubilant squeals of laughter.

Killer might have kept on south till he reached Mexico. Might have turned back time all the way to the Aztecs and taken his revenge on Montezuma for them fire-breathing peppers. But he didn't. Didn't get that far. He ran out of oats.

Gregory saw the outline of a town only a moment before his body was stung by an icy coldness. The cold shot up his trousers, sliced under his shirt . . . shivered his timbers. When his toes hit upon something solid, he pushed off for warmer climes. The first thing he saw was Maw, flailing circles like a winged top.

"Water!" Maw screamed. "Man the lifeboats. Women and children first!"

Killer had found his water, all right. A whole huge trough of it. He'd braked just a spit in front of the cedar-planked tub, toppling all three riders into the drink. Salvation at hand, the horse plunged his head over the top and was now eye deep in wet, swilling like a parched hippo.

Gregory forged his way through the rapidly receding water, tossing Maw to the ground before tumbling out himself. The two stood all adrip, eyes feasting on the sight before them.

What they saw was a town not unlike Sharpesville — with storefronts, hitchin' posts, and rickety sidewalks separated by a street of hardened earth. Shops called attention to themselves with signs advertising Saloon, General Merchandise, Hotel, and Land Claims. But it was the two words prefixing each sign that swelled Maw with pride and led Gregory to exclaim: "Flat Rock, Maw. We done it!"

This announcement was followed by a loud,

squishy slurp as Killer sucked up the last of the water. He'd guzzled the whole tub dry. Looked it too — so gorged his legs had all but disappeared. Lifting his head, the horse stared daggers at Gregory before sidestepping off to ease himself down on his bloated belly for a well-deserved rest.

Gregory checked Sy's watch. The watch — still warm from the ride — had stopped at exactly five o'clock. Maw took this to be a good sign. But she held off celebrating. "Never count your babes before they're birthed," she told Gregory. "We got the town right, but the year and date still need proving. Better scout it out."

Gregory took off like a bullet, spraying water as he went. He headed straight for the office of the *Flat Rock Gazette*. There weren't many people around, it being late in the day. But when he passed Miss Lucy's dress shop, Hefty Fashions for the Full-Figured, he had to zigzag out of the path of two women who were just then exiting.

"Howdy, ma'ams."

"Howdy, yourself," said one of the ladies. "A mite chilly for swimming, don't you think? You'll get a lickin' for sure when your mom finds out."

Gregory kept right on running, a smile lighting his face. "Maw knows," he called behind him. "She nearly drowned, herself."

Reaching the *Gazette*'s window, Gregory held the stitch in his side as he scanned the one-page paper taped to the glass. He gave a holler when he saw the date, then fixed his sights on a small paragraph near the bottom. He could hardly keep his feet still as his mouth moved around the words. MEANEY BIRTH IMMINENT. *Dolores and Clyde Meaney eagerly await . . .* He read the whole thing twice just so he'd remember.

"Hoppin' horned toads!" he yelled. "Maw!"

Now if you're smart, you may have realized that something — someone — was missing. Maw had the same sensation as she watched Gregory skedaddle for the news office. Shaking the water from her feathers, she cocked her head, wondering if time travel affects a person's memory. She hummed herself a few bars of "Yankee Doodle" just to be sure everything upstairs was in working order. When she came to the part about "Riding on a pony," she did some quick counting. That's when it struck her.

"The Mean One," she said. "We lost him!"

After surveying the ground around her, Maw shot to the rim of the now-waterless trough, where a shocking sight met her eyes. What she saw, stretched out a good four feet below, was the Mean One, who didn't look at all well. There was a bluish cast to his face. And his lips were locked open in an angry snarl — as if the man's last communion with the world had been to curse the very idea of a bath. From his forehead bulged a purple knot of swelling. The knot had already reached walnut size and was still growing. Maw winced when she noticed the indentation on the top of the trough's opposite wall where the big guy must have hit.

"Hate to see it end this way," she murmured. "It's an awful thing to die without a heart, even if you have been overly nasty."

Suddenly one of the long stringy hairs under the Mean One's nose stirred. Or at least Maw thought it stirred. And she hopped down onto the giant's chest for a closer look. Her weight, little though it was, caused an explosion of water to burst from the Mean One's mouth. Maw dashed back to the rim of the trough in order to safely watch the display . . . the high-arcing geyser catching the sun and scattering rainbow colors like sparks.

It was a pretty sight, and Maw was kind of sorry to see it end, the fountain diminishing in strength till it was nothing but a trickle. Abruptly, the Mean One's chest began to rise and fall ever so slightly, causing Maw to shout, "Heck, you ain't dead, after all. Just unconscious!"

That's when Gregory arrived, out of breath, with the news.

"It's like you figured, Maw — 1881. April first. No fooling. I read it plain as day. And there's a birth about to take place. Said so in the paper — Ouch!" he added, seeing the Mean One's forehead. "Is he — ?"

"Alive," said Maw. "Barely. But we'll need some help if we're to get him to his birth."

Wouldn't you know it, help was already on the way. Coming in the form of a mule-drawn wagon careening nearly out of control, steered by a man mostly bones and black fabric. The man had been sitting quite bored at the second-floor window of his place of business when he'd seen Killer streak into town. Pressing his pointed nose to the fly-stained window, the man had studied the scene for a full minute before crying, "Customers! What luck!"

In his haste, the man tumbled down half a flight of stairs. Nearly broke his neck. But didn't. It was his spectacles that got broke. That's why the wagon was rollicking from one side of the street to the other. The man couldn't see worth a plugged nickel without his specs.

Maw leaped for Gregory's shoulder as the man managed to stop the cart with a loud "Whoooaaaa!" Jumping down, the man doffed his top hat to reveal a bald head, smooth as an egg, fringed by spidery black hair.

"Terrible . . . just terrible," he blurted. "Saw the whole thing. Would have been here sooner if I hadn't lost my specs." He squinted toward the trough. "Such a tragedy when a loved one kicks the buck — I mean, is taken so sudden."

Maw's eyes darted from the man to the back of the wagon. For there, gaping lidless and wafting a scent of new-cut pine, were several coffins of varying sizes. Gregory took in the uneven lettering painted along the wagon's side wall.

S.A.D. UNDERTAKING

AFFORDABLE BURIALS

SAME-DAY SERVICE

BURY YOUR SORROW BEFORE TOMORROW

"Samuel Albert Deeter at your service," the man said. "I put 'em under without a blunder." Pulling a card from his coat pocket, he clapped it into Gregory's palm with a hearty handshake. "Special today — ten percent off."

"But," said Gregory, "we don't need no — "

"Wait!" cried Maw. "Better let the man advise us . . . we being strangers to these parts and all."

The undertaker showed no alarm at Maw's gift of speech. In fact, he was relieved. Having already calculated how much richer he'd be at the end of the day, he was glad to know there was an adult present for billing purposes.

"Warms ma heart to know the boy won't be left an orphan," he told Maw with a gracious nod.

"We come a long distance," Maw said. "To witness a birth on this very day. Hadn't planned on a burial to boot."

"Such a pity. To gain one and lose one on the same day. At least it comes out even."

He was about to cackle at his own joke when his eyebrows arrowed up suddenly.

"Why, it's Dolores and Clyde Meaney who be birthin' today! Doc Hazard left for their place not an hour ago." His eyes met over his nose with the thought. "You must be relations!"

Maw avowed that they were. Then nodded to Gregory. "Leastways, the Mean One is," she said with a wink.

"It'll be my unhappy task to take a gander at the deceased," Samuel said.

Strutting forward, he ran smack into the side of the trough, then rubbed the pain from his knees with a mumbling of words that didn't sound like any prayer Gregory knew. When he looked inside, he gave a gasp.

"Ugly — I mean, that's a Meaney, all right. Spittin' image of Clyde." He squinted harder. "But that's a man. Only relation Clyde has is his twin sister, Iris, who left Flat Rock years ago."

Gregory needed no coaching from Maw to know they'd stumbled onto a piece of luck.

"That there *is* Iris," he said.

Samuel flinched. "You mean she took up gunslinging?"

"Yes, sir. Could spin and shoot with the best."

"Don't say . . . don't say. Course I ain't seen Iris in a coon's age. Time seems to have gone hard on her. Is that a beard she's sportin'?"

"And let that be a lesson to us all," Maw rushed to say. "Not to believe every sales pitch you hear. Poor Iris bought a bottle of hair thickener from a traveling peddler who swore by the stuff. Her hair had begun to thin some on top — maybe you can relate. Anyway, that potion didn't do a thing for her head, but it put a right thick coat around her chin."

"I never trust them fellows, myself," Samuel replied, rubbing his baldness. He sniffed, screwing up his face at the Mean One's smell, which would take more than a single bath to erase. "We best get moving. Ol' Iris is already starting to stink."

"She'll need a pretty dress to wear to her burial," Maw added. "Them men's clothes are just traveling fare. If'n she knew she was gonna die, she most likely would have packed a decent gingham. Prob'ly forgot to change her underwear, too."

Samuel coughed politely into his fist. "There is the tiny matter of a fee, ma'am."

Gregory and Maw had never had any use for money. But they were good at trading. "You might just as well take Iris's forty-fives as payment," Gregory said. "She won't be needing them anymore."

Samuel's defective eyes lit up at that. "Why, that should just about cover it. I'll have ol' Iris fixed up pretty as a new bride. And I'll ride you poor bereaved folks right up to Clyde's doorstep. Then we can put Iris to rest." He shook his head. "It'll be a sad reunion for Clyde."

"That it will," said Maw. "But it never pays to hide the truth."

"Never," Samuel echoed, figuring the two guns were worth a good six or seven burials at the least.

8. Zenith

The first thing Samuel did — after proudly strapping on his new guns — was to run to the saloon for help. He came back with two men, both a little tipsy. Swaying before the trough, the men paid their respects.

"Used to sit beside Iris in school when we was kids," one of the men said. "Nearly took out my jaw with a right hook when I suggested she start shavin'."

"Me and Iris went to the graduation — *hic* — dance together," the other said. "That's how I got ma limp."

Samuel secured a rope around the Mean One's chest, and the three men managed to pull the body from the trough. Grunting, they dragged the corpse to the wagon, then climbed onto the bed for better leverage. With a mighty heave, they had the body standing upright. Gregory pushed from the ground as on "three" the men strained against the rope, popping a goodly amount of sweat.

Maw had been fretting that the Mean One might spoil everything by waking too soon. She needn't have. For whatever steps toward consciousness the Mean One had taken were quickly retraced as his head thunked into the foot of the largest coffin.

"*Hic* — oops!"

"What was that?"

"What?"

"A groan . . . sounded like it come from — "

"Dead people don't groan," Samuel said. "So you needn't scare yerselfs. That's just her insides settlin'."

Gregory climbed aboard, and each of the four took a limb. The body wobbled upward.

"Ouch . . . my lumbago."

"Swing 'er this way a jigger."

"Now!"

A cloud of pine dust flew up as the body thudded home. Samuel snorted the dust clear from his nostrils. "Thanks, boys. She'll sleep tight in there." He paid the men a dime apiece for their trouble, and the men — sore but sobered — headed back to their bar stools to tell how Iris had met her fate.

Next Samuel visited Miss Lucy's Hefty Fashions, returning with a red polka-dot dress and matching bonnet.

"Last year's design," he told Maw. "But it was the biggest available. Miss Lucy was about to turn it into an awning for the front of the shop."

The high-waisted dress had a linen collar studded with tiny pink bows. Maw turned wistful. "Never had a little girl to dress up cute and sassy. It's darling."

Gregory started to pry off one of the Mean One's boots, intending to strip him down, but Maw vetoed the idea. "No tellin' what unpleasantness may be lurking inside those shoes," she said. So they just buttoned the dress around him instead.

When Gregory had tied the bonnet's ribbon ties into a knot beneath the Mean One's furry chin, he asked, "Think we should take Killer along?"

"If he'll come," Maw answered. "Hate to lose sight of our ticket home."

Gregory had just the idea for rousing Killer. He yelled "SHERIFF!" as loud as he could. The horse struggled to his feet, head whipping from side to—side in search of a badge. He found none, but appeared glad to be elevated again. Thinking the previous indignities to be but a horrific nightmare, he stepped wide legged to the wagon, where Gregory tethered him to the back with Samuel's rope.

Samuel meantime had draped some tattered black bunting along the wagon's flanks, turning the cart into a regular hearse. Then Maw and Gregory hopped in the back to keep the Mean One company, and Samuel, having taken his position up front, put a little spit shine to the brim of his hat before flicking the reins.

The funeral rode straight through town, causing folks to step into doorways and to peep from behind curtains, heads bowed. Samuel informed Maw that a song came for free with the deal, and he broke into a forceful rendering of "Rock of Ages" that had both Maw and Gregory hitchin' their shoulders to cover their ears.

Outside of town, the road snaked narrow and rocky. Gregory held one hand to the coffin and the other to the side of the wagon to steady himself. "The Mean One'll be a mite angry to wake and find himself sportin' a dress," he told Maw.

"It'll ruffle his feathers some," Maw replied. "But that's a chance we got to take. He needs to see that he was born with a heart. Might soften his edges. The man's been at war with himself for a long time . . . and has caused a trainload of trouble because of it.

"Life be fraught with chances," she added with a sigh. "I learned that when I came back from breakfast that day to find you in my nest."

"You took a chance raisin' me, didn't you?" Gregory said.

"It's a powerful responsibility raisin' a child. I was afraid I'd get it wrong."

Reaching across the open coffin, Gregory smoothed an out-of-place feather on her neck. "You done perfect," he said.

"Best chance I ever took," said Maw.

* * *

Maw wasn't the only mother in Flat Rock teary-eyed just then. Not a mile away was another mom who felt a similar stirring.

"He's . . . he's prettier than an Easter ham," Dolores Meaney said, folding her new babe into her arms for the first time.

Her husband, Clyde, a towering tree of a man, was flushed with fatherly pride. "And twice as big," he said. "He's a Meaney, all right. How much you think he weighs, Doc?"

"Plenty," Doc Hazard replied, still awed that Dolores — large though she was — had carried such a load to term. "Course my expertise is mainly in veterinary medicine. But that's the biggest hog — I mean boy — I've ever birthed."

"Handsome too, eh, Doc?" Clyde asked through a tooth-missing grin. "Ain't he the handsomest boy you've ever set eyes on?"

Doc fumbled with the stethoscope around his neck. The stethoscope — two lengths of hose whose bottom ends were stuffed into the neck of a battered tin funnel — had the sour smell of whiskey mash about it. Prob'ly because when Doc wasn't making house calls he was making some of Flat Rock's finest moonshine. Clyde's question made Doc wish for a good snort of white lightnin' even then.

"Never seen a babe with a five-o'clock stubble on its chin," he said. "The boy'll turn heads, all right."

As coincidence would have it, a head was already turned in the new babe's direction. The head belonged to Zenith Kopetsky, who lived in a broken-down, woebegone caravan just a stone's throw from the fork in the road that led to the Meaneys' parcel of land. Zenith made what living she could telling fortunes. She was good at it too — reading palms, tea leaves, bathtub rings . . . even hangnails if she had a mind to. She could tell a person's shoe size just from the width of his brow. Knew from the shape of an earlobe if a body'd be filthy rich or dirt poor.

Zenith had been sitting on an overturned crate in the doorway to her caravan, slicing up some near-to-rotted turnips for supper, when she felt the prickling sensation that swung her head toward the Meaneys'. "The babe be borned," she spoke low, shuddering the knife point into her thumb.

Flinching, she studied the hurt with her one good eye. Then lifted the eyepatch of the other for a second opinion. A tear-shaped bubble of blood rose from the cut. Zenith's tongue shot out lizardy to erase the bad sign. Didn't take but a fraction of her second sight to realize the new babe spelled trouble.

Leaping from the crate, she grabbed her shawl from its nail hook and pulled it tight around her. Below, across the sloping field that led to the road, she spied the outline of a wagon, her nose twitching at the unusual smell. When the wagon grew more vivid, she saw it was Samuel's hearse. "But that ain't death I'm sniffin'," she told herself. "It's meanness. And it lives."

At once Zenith rushed to the back of the caravan, her good eye squinting as she swept a gnarled finger past jars of skunk cabbage, valerian root, and dried coltsfoot. Her finger stopped stiff before a small brown vial. Wrenching the vial from its clutch of cobwebs, she stormed out into the daylight, her frail legs taking her across the field, her thick skirts picking up a sampling of every seed and stickweed along the way. She converged on the road fork just as Samuel was steering his mule up the Meaneys' rutted drive.

Samuel raised himself important when he saw Zenith standing tuckered by the road. He'd learned over the years that folks couldn't help noseying up to a hearse for the latest burial gossip. "Iris Meaney it be," he called. "Poor girl. Should have had more sense than to butt heads with a four-inch cedar plank."

Zenith's face was too scored with wrinkles for Samuel to notice she was grinning. But she was. She'd always thought Samuel to be the closest thing to a fool she'd meet in this lifetime. When the wagon creaked past, Zenith stepped straight in its wake, drawing back her arm. Gregory and Maw both waved back to be polite. That's when Zenith let go with the vial tucked in her fist.

Gregory saw the bottle split the dusted air. He quick-moved his hand in front of his face, the bottle slapping sudden into his palm.

"She's either limberin' up her arm for a carnival throw or she's right unneighborly," he told Maw. "Good shot, though, for a lady with but one eye."

Maw hadn't taken her sights off the strange woman who now took to following behind the wagon at a slow but steady clip. "Better open the bottle," she said. "That old gal knows something."

Gregory popped the cork, his head jerking back. "Phew! Smelling salts, Maw. Got the scent of a three-day-dead catfish."

"Thought there was something fishy about her. I'll wager she intends for us to use the salts on the Mean One."

"But how could she know?"

The hearse topped a rise in the road and Samuel pointed to a squat cabin up ahead. "That's the place," he said all too happily.

Maw took a quick gander at their destination, then turned back to where Zenith — outdistanced by Samuel's mule — had grown smaller.

"Makes no matter how she knows," Maw continued. "What matters is that we let Killer roam free for a spell. For his own protection. No telling what'll happen once the big guy comes to. When we reach the house, we'll use the salts to wake ol' Iris here. Then we best make tracks ourselves."

Gregory felt the excitement power through his body. Scuttling for the tailgate, he quick untied Killer, who wasted no time locating a bush of fresh-blossomed sage to munch.

Samuel pulled the wagon to a whoa directly in front of the cabin. "Always wanted to give one of my customers a farewell salute," he said, unholstering his new guns.

Lifting both pieces high, he let fire.

9. Sis!

Inside the cabin, Dolores's scream staggered the rafters and sent a painful reminder to Doc that he was still plugged to his stethoscope. Babe in arms, Dolores took to the air, diving for cover under the swaybacked four-poster in the corner. Clyde and Doc hit the deck an instant later, dusting a few floorboards of their own.

"Some hunter gone loco," Doc said, grimacing as he unsheathed a splinter from his nose.

"On his last hunt," replied Clyde, who was already crawling for the door where his shotgun lay propped and waiting.

Samuel's salute ran out of bullets just as Gregory passed the salts under the Mean One's nose for the fifth time. Gregory watched the big hairy nostrils quiver and the curtainy eyelids snap open.

"Catfish!" the giant spluttered, his hand swinging up to touch the knot on his forehead. "I been hit by a catfish. I see stars!"

Of course it wasn't stars he was seeing. It was the brim of his cute and sassy bonnet. And when his eyes focused full, he yelled, "Dots! Polka dots! What the — "

"Now don't get nasty," Gregory hurried a whisper. "You're home. This be Flat Rock, and — "

"Save yourself, boy!" Maw cried as she took wing.

Gregory leaped the wagon's side rail just as the Mean One felt the coffin's crampness. There was a groaning of nails and a sudden crackling of wood as the coffin's walls exploded from their seams.

"Don't shoot!" Samuel shouted when the cabin door burst open to reveal the twin barrels of Clyde's gun leveled at his Adam's apple.

"Samuel!" Doc said, poking his head from behind Clyde's shoulder. "You about scared the skin off'n us . . . and Dolores with a new babe, too."

"Didn't mean to rile you none," blustered Samuel. "It's woeful tidings I bring. Got her boxed right here in the back. Ready for your good-byes."

Turning to point out the meaning to his words, Samuel saw the polka-dotted bonnet rise from the flattened remnants of coffin. The undertaker's face switched color like a chameleon skittering through a rainbow, finally fixing on white.

"She's . . . she's . . . she's risen! Jumpin' juniper berries — A GHOST!"

The Mean One took only a second to study his new wardrobe. Then spun to all fours, looking like a demented grizzly who'd just unclipped some lady's Sunday best from a backyard clothesline.

"A DRESS!" he bellowed, eyes tacked to the horrified Samuel. "Why, I'll rip your teeth out!"

Samuel didn't wait to have his teeth ripped out. Snatching up the reins, he lashed a week's worth of pasture dust from his mule's hide, yelling, "Yee-ah . . . Yee-ah!"

Gregory had once seen Phineas T. amaze a crowd by whipping a tablecloth out from beneath a dinner setting for four. The cloth pulled off clean as a whistle, barely shaking the plates and crystal.

That's the way it was as the hearse shot forward. It left the Mean One in mid charge, nothing but air to support him. Furious, he lashed out at the passing wagon, clasping a paw to the tailgate even as gravity took hold. He hit the ground like an anchor, jerking both wagon and mule to a most sudden stop.

What didn't stop was Samuel.

"Look!" Gregory said as Samuel went sailing forward from his seat bench.

Maw wasn't one to waste a chance for educatin'. "A body in motion tends to stay in motion," she said.

Samuel didn't stay in motion for long. He bottomed out hard atop the braying mule. There —

crazy with fear at being so proximate to a real-live ghost — he urged the animal on with a flurry of knees and elbows. Neither mule nor man made a lick of progress, though. For, having found his footing, the Mean One now clamped his other hand to the tailgate. With both arms stretched full, he gritted his hugesome teeth and pulled harder against the mule's forward strain.

Well, it was a stand-off. A stalemate. A real tug-o'-war.

From their front-row seats, Gregory and Maw thought the opposing forces might split the wagon in two. What happened instead was the wagon's wheels started spinning right there in place. Spun so fast that the axles overheated, sending out a cloud of smoke. It was the smoke that caused the Mean One to cough and release his grip, springing the wagon forth like a lima bean launched from a slingshot.

Gregory lifted a hand in farewell to Samuel as the hearse blazed a new trail through Flat Rock's hinterlands, accompanied by the undertaker's hysterical *Yee-ah*s.

The Mean One shook his fist at the receding wagon, swearing a streak. Clyde, who'd had his gun pointed all this time waiting for something stationary to shoot at, recognized the cuss words at once as those he and his sister had practiced in their youth whenever they'd hammered a finger or got stung by a bee. As the smoke and dust cleared,

Clyde got a better look at the person still raging after the disappeared hearse. The blunt profile and broad shoulders were unmistakable.

"Sis!" he hollered. "Sis! Can it be?

"Honey, look," he called to Dolores, who appeared at the door with her bundle of babe. "Look who come to share in our birthing joy."

The Mean One blinked so hard and fast he nearly produced Flat Rock's first electric current fifty years before its time. "Ma?" he mouthed. "Pa?"

"Iris!" Dolores said jubilantly, holding up the baby. "We've a son!"

This time the Mean One managed to speak his thought out loud. What he said was a single word. A question, really.

"Norbert?"

Dolores nearly dropped the bundle in surprise. "Why, we only just named the boy. It's Norbert, all right. You're somethin', Iris."

"Ain't she, though?" said Clyde, rushing over to clap his sister on the back. "Even put on a new dress for the occasion. Well, come on in and give your dogs a rest, Sis. We'll fix a poultice for that nasty lump you got hangin' from your forehead. And have ourselves a toast. Got a jug of fresh stump water, only a week old, just waitin' to be uncorked."

Gregory stepped forward then, clearing the frog from his throat. "I'm a friend of Iris's, sir," he said. "We've traveled a healthy distance together."

"Any friend of Iris's be a friend of ours," Clyde answered. "Y'all come in, too. It's a great day!"

* 80 *

And so, with Dolores proudly leading the way, and the Mean One as confounded as a tick on a bearskin rug, they filed inside. All except Maw, who flew to the edge of the dirt yard, where Zenith had been secretly watching the proceedings with interest.

Maw found the old woman on her knees, bent over a scattering of polished bones.

"Rattlesnake knuckles," Zenith said before Maw could frame the question.

"Didn't know rattlesnakes even had knuckles," Maw said.

Zenith looked up. "That's what makes these so special."

"What do you read from them?" Maw asked.

"They say it ain't natural you folks being here. They say that there polka-dotted fella and the babe be one and the same." She scooped the bones to her bosom and grunted herself up. "But I don't need no bones to know that Flat Rock be doomed 'cause of that Norbert boy."

"No hope for Flat Rock . . . that's a fact," Maw said. "It's the farthest future we be aimin' to fix. That's why we come. Will you help us?"

Zenish flipped up her patch, the creamy white marble of her glass eye glittering pinbeams of sun.

"I'll see what I can do," she said.

10. It Beats

Still a trifle weak at the knees from giving birth, Dolores eased herself into one of the chairs around the cabin's table. Clyde fluffed a bed pillow behind her. "Now don't you worry none, honey — Doc and I will take good care of our guests."

"You bet," said Doc. "I'll git the stump water. My insides could use a good spring cleanin'."

All the shooting and hollering hadn't disturbed Baby Norbert in the least. He slept tight in his mother's arms, his fat fuzzy cheeks billowing like mainsails before each snore.

The Mean One stood stiff as a drainspout just inside the door. It was like he'd run into a glass wall. Like he was seeing the home of his youth through a window in some traveling museum show. When his hand reached out to find air instead of glass, the emotion broke hard over him. Gregory grabbed his wrist, reminding him to breathe.

"Iris," called Clyde. "Come on, girl . . . take a load off your feet."

"Ain't her feet that's the trouble," Gregory said, covering for the Mean One's shock. "It's her head. She banged it pretty good."

Swiping a fingerful of salve from a tin on the cluttered sideboard, Clyde rushed over.

"Guaranteed to heal," he said, planting the goo on the Mean One's forehead. "Got the recipe from old Zenith herself. Made from gen-u-ine gopher parts."

At first Gregory thought it was the aroma of gen-u-ine gopher parts causing him to see double. Then he realized what he was seeing was Clyde together with his grown-up son — the two giants standing just a nose length apart. Except for a few more missing teeth and a hint of gray in Clyde's whiskers, father and son looked to be mirror images of each other.

As for Clyde, he hadn't been nose to nose with his twin sister since Iris had struck out to make her fortune by joining the circus.

"Don't the Lord work in strange ways," he said, shaking his head. "That beard of yours turned out to be a blessin' after all." And he couldn't resist laying a big wet kiss on the Mean One's lips.

The Mean One jerked back as if scorpion stung. Truth was, he hadn't been kissed like that in years. Not since he was a boy. Not since he'd come in from a day's play to leap into his pap's loving arms. "Daddy," he said, his gruff voice suddenly tenderized with longing.

"Why, you're the first to call me such, Iris," Clyde answered. "It sure do have a nice ring to it."

"All set," Doc called from the table where he'd poured out four glasses of amber-colored stump water from a gallon jug. Considered a delicacy, the water was really rainwater allowed to age in the stumps of dead trees. After a few days of aging, the water was carefully collected along with whatever creatures, both swimmers and nonswimmers — alive and not — were found therein. Heavily sugared and eye-droppered with licorice extract for taste, the resulting tonic was said to be good for both body and soul.

Clyde sprang for the table, and Gregory gave the Mean One a push in the same direction. One look at the glass Doc handed him, and Gregory recalled how he wasn't all that fond of stump water. Nose wrinkling, the boy began picking out the needles, egg sacs, and bug husks floating on the water's surface.

"You addled, son?" said Doc. "You'll spoil the flavor, removin' the natural spices like that."

"Actually," said Gregory, "I was just thinking how a glass of milk would go down mighty easy 'bout now . . . I mean, if it ain't too much bother."

"Why, we got plenty of sweet milk," Clyde said, ladling up a fresh glass from a bucket near the hearth.

As the rest of the drinks were passed around, something shuffled into the open doorway, dimming the cabin's light.

"Zenith!" said Clyde. "We was hoping you'd drop by. Be much obliged if you'd give us a reading on our new little critter."

Gregory was glad to see Maw standing at the old woman's feet. Though he knew Maw would never run out on him, he'd been more than a little nervous at her absence.

"There's that bird again," Dolores said. "The same that was outside. Better shoot it, dear."

Clyde made a move for his gun.

"No!" yelled Gregory. "That's Maw. She's with Iris and me."

"I once knew a fellow who had a crow for a pet," Doc said. "You'd have thought the bird was almost human the way it learned to talk. Does yours talk?"

Gregory swallowed a laugh. "Sometimes too much," he said.

"Only when her boy gets uppity and looks to be in need of a good tongue-lashing," Maw countered. She scampered to the table and fluttered herself up. "Stump tonic, eh?" she said, eyeing Gregory's original glass in which a couple of tadpoles were synchronizing their tail strokes. "Don't mind if I do . . . I'm as dry as a barnful of last year's hay."

Zenith strode sternly to the table, the hem of her shawl bouncing behind her. Dressed mostly in black and bent over at the shoulders, she bore a strong resemblance to a crow herself. Keeping her one good eye on the babe, she drained the glass of stump water Doc had planned for himself.

"You asked for a reading and I'll give it," she said after smacking her lips. "The kid won't be much to look at. But he'll be a good boy and make his parents proud . . . up until the time — "

Maw could see no reason why Dolores and Clyde should have such a happy occasion spoiled with talk of future horrors. And she cut off Zenith with a squawk that climbed three registers of sound, ending with a note so high and pure that underneath its patch, Zenith's glass eye sang like a tuning fork.

Baby Norbert awoke with the clamor, coming out of his sleep with a gurgly drool . . . his sausage fingers groping the air. He kept his eyelids pressed shut, as if wishing himself back to the quiet dark of his mother's womb.

"To Norbert!" Clyde said proudly, lifting his glass to celebrate Zenith's forecast. "He's a keeper."

"Too big to throw back," Doc said before taking a pull of stump water direct from the jug.

"May he have a heart of gold," Dolores added.

The Mean One was in mid swallow when he heard the word *heart*. The word brought a knifelike pain to his chest. Gagging, he swung his hand to the pain, a goodly share of his drink splashing onto his dress. "Heart!" he said. "Heart!"

"Her ticker's goin'!" Clyde yelled, jumping from his chair and racing for the gopher salve.

"Boil some water," shouted Doc. "Stand her up in a fresh bed of hay."

"She ain't *calvin'!*" Dolores said. "The poor woman's tryin' to tell us somethin'."

Maw nodded so strenuously to Gregory she nearly threw herself into a faint.

"What Iris means to tell," Gregory hurried to say, "is that she'd like to listen to the baby's heart through Doc's instrument there. Wouldn't ya, Iris?"

Amid the pain in his chest and the burning rush of stump water that had been forced up his nose, the Mean One could only blink in reply.

Doc knew a *yes* blink when he saw one. "Well, why didn't you say so?" he said, tossing his stethoscope to Gregory who wasted no time plugging the hoses into the Mean One's hairy ears. Tugging the big man closer to Dolores and the babe, Gregory eagerly laid the wide of the funnel to the infant's chest.

It was quiet, then. So quiet you could hear the termites working on the cabin's walls. The Mean One's jaw hung slack as he strained to listen. Suddenly his brows rose in surprise. Real surprise. Like he'd stepped barefoot on a sleeping snake.

"It beats!" he said. "It beats! I can hear it!"

Doc wasn't all that impressed. "Course it beats," he said. "Hearts mostly do. Leastways, the live ones do. Learned that in veterinary school."

It was then that Baby Norbert decided to take his first look at the world. His eyelids pricked open to see the Mean One's huge whiskered face hovering over him. Of course it could have been the Mean One's breath that set the babe to wailing. But Maw said later it was most likely the sight of what he was soon to become that caused Norbert to scream so loud, the Mean One had to tear the hoses from his ears in self-defense. So frightened was the babe, he flailed himself right out of Dolores's grasp. Swam a good two feet in the air before Clyde caught him up like you'd catch a sack of flour tossed your way.

"Now, now," Clyde clucked, trying to quiet the babe. "That ain't nothin'. It's just your Auntie Iris."

Knowing for sure he had been born with a heart caused the Mean One to go a tad misty-eyed.

"No need to get yourself upset, Iris," Dolores said. "The boy's just a mite skittish around strangers is all."

"And most likely hungry," Maw added, figuring they'd accomplished what they'd come for. "It's clear we've overstayed our visit. The boy needs some privacy with his mother to take his nourishment."

Dolores agreed it was prob'ly so as she took the still-bawling babe from Clyde. Gregory laid the stethoscope on the table next to Doc, who rumbled a licorice-laced snore, the man's afternoon nap long overdue.

Outside, the evening sun had turned the scrubby landscape a deep gold. Clyde clapped the Mean One's back over and over, saying what a joyful surprise it had all been. He made Maw and Gregory promise to visit whenever Iris and the circus played Flat Rock again.

Gregory retrieved Killer from his pasturing, and our heroes started down the drive. They weren't going far. Only to Zenith's, the old woman making good on her promise to help.

Zenith led the way, with Maw riding her shoulder. The Mean One, dazed and weakened by the rising and falling of so much emotion in so short a time, rode Killer. Gregory ambled along beside the horse. "See?" he told the Mean One. "You was born with a heart, after all. Don't that make you feel good?"

The Mean One held a hand to his chest as he swayed back and forth in the saddle, his bonnet teetering from side to side on his head. "I was a pretty babe," he said. "With a heart."

Gregory figured one out of two wasn't half bad. "We'll find that heart of yours," he offered encouragingly, "if it's the last thing we do."

"Might just be," Zenith murmured. She plunged a hand into the pocket of her skirt and shook the rattlesnake bones there. "You'll need some luck, that's for sure," she told Maw.

Maw begged to differ. "It's courage and smarts that have brought us this far and courage and smarts that'll take us the rest of the way," she said. She paused long enough to think of Sharpesville. It seemed a long distance away.

"Twenty-five years to be exact," Zenith said.

Maw didn't care for having her thoughts read like that. She cleared her mind by looking straight down the road. Then she reconsidered.

"Better give those bones another shake," she said.

11. Foxfire

The path leading up to Zenith's caravan was signposted every few feet.

"So's a person won't miss what I'm offerin'," Zenith said.

Maw marveled at the woman's keen business sense. Gregory read each sign aloud as they passed. *Fortunes Told. Remedies Sold. Charms, Tinctures, & Ointments. Strictly Confidenshal. A Penny Will Buy You Plenny.* He had trouble deciphering the meaning of the last sign. "What's *Burma Shave*?" he asked.

"Beats me," Zenith answered. "Saw it in a dream once. Seemed important."

The Mean One had recovered close to his old

self by the time they reached the van. He eyed Zenith's home for only a moment before concluding he'd seen nicer-lookin' rats' nests.

Dismounting, he aimed himself into a bed of purple petunias, where he proceeded to kick off the heads of those few flowers that weren't crushed by his initial drop. The destruction appeared to make him feel even better. With a satisfied grunt, he collapsed into the shade of a sun-blackened pine to take his usual before-supper nap.

"He sure is a disagreeable lout," Zenith said. "If ya want, I can take a stab at him with my turnip knife. Just sharpened it today."

"Maw and I don't put much stock in violence," Gregory said. "Besides, we made a bargain to help the big guy out."

Zenith shrugged off her disappointment. "Well, then," she said. "First things first. . . . I never work on an empty stomach." She led Gregory and Maw to the back of the caravan, where a garden lay full to bursting with herbs and vegetables. There she started cutting from a patch of collard greens, planning to add the greens to the turnips she'd been working on for supper.

Impressed though he was by the garden, Gregory was even more struck by the smell. The stink came from a large compost heap set off to one side. The heap held a mix of rotting tumbleweeds, artichoke leaves, cactus rinds, eggshells, coffee grounds, and what looked to be clumps of dried oatmeal with strange green fuzzies growing from them. A pitchfork stuck straight out from the mess.

"The dirt around here ain't worth much," Zenith said. "So I make my own soil. You get used to the smell."

Gregory held his breath and used the pitchfork to turn some of the garbage over. Underneath was a layer of the finest soil he'd even seen . . . rich and black and crawling with worms thick as fingers.

Maw blew a fervent sigh at the sight. "Now I *am* hungry," she said. "When's chow?"

They ate quiet, sitting around the front steps of the caravan and watching the shadows lengthen as the sun dropped behind them. Maw didn't care much for the greens and turnips. But she ate more than her share of Zenith's corn pone and looked forward to spearing a couple of them giant worms out back for dessert.

The Mean One ate by himself under the pine, using his hands for spoons and flattening any ants that dared make a move toward his plate. He'd gone into a real frenzy when he'd woken from his catnap to finally discover his guns were missing — ripped his dress to pieces and stomped the bonnet underfoot till it was a thready pulp. So hard did he complain about losing his gunslinging hat that Zenith gave him an old straw one of her own, which sort of fit once he fisted a hole through the top.

"I thought he'd be happy," Gregory said softly

as he watched the Mean One pound another ant. "You'd think he'd be glad to learn he was born with a heart."

"Knowing you lost something you once had hurts worse than not having the thing in the first place," Maw said. She recounted how Sy had snapped his new five-dollar fish pole over his knee and tossed it into the Pustulli.

"He'd been stalking this big old catfish for weeks," she told Zenith. "He fin'ly hooked it. But the fish squirmed free. The poor man couldn't bear the loss. If the fish hadn't bit, Sy would still have his pole . . . still be stalking that fish without a care in the world."

"I know all about losing things and hurtin'," Zenith said. "Lost my first husband to Eunice Craddock in a poker game. I was short on cash at the time, and the man was a no-count, so I bet 'im. Didn't think a thing about it at the time. Missed him bad, though, when I learned he stumbled on a vein of gold while diggin' for night crawlers up around Horse Thief Lake."

Darkness was settling in fast. Maw said they'd best get on with what they come for. Zenith ducked into the caravan and returned with a lamp whose light flickered yellow bands and lit up the old woman's face like a jack-o'-lantern. She set the lamp on the ground so they could all sit around it.

"It's you we'll be talkin' about," Maw called to the Mean One. "So you might as well join us."

Scuffing his boots and kicking up a fair amount of dust, the Mean One lumbered over. With a scowl, he dropped himself into the circle, and Zenith began.

"The way Maw tells it, y'all want a reading on Norbert's future. You need to know when he lost his heart so's you can recover it."

"I was a pretty babe," the Mean One muttered same as before. "With a heart."

Zenith nodded. "One out of two ain't half bad," she said. She freed her arms from her shawl and brought both hands up to her eye patch. Lifting the patch with the fingers of one hand, she used the thumb of the other to spring her glass eye from its socket. The eye came out with a soft ripping sound, and she caught it up in her palm.

Gregory thought it was like Zenith was wishing herself luck at a craps shoot, the way she blew so fiercely through her fingers onto the eye. She hummed real deep and meaningful between breaths, as if speaking directly to the eye for help. Finally, she slid her hand outward toward the lamp, unfolding her fingers one at a time.

The eye wobbled in the woman's withered palm before stopping dead. Gregory looked from the eye to the vacated socket, wondering if it hurt. Maw gave a whistle to see the eye standing free of Zenith's head. The Mean One touched his own eyes, just to be sure they were still where they should be.

Zenith's good eye arrowed in on the disembod-ied other. "What I see," she said, her voice low and spooky, "is the babe Norbert growing like a weed. Kinda clumsy 'cause of his size. But he's ever help-ful and kind. I see him making his parents proud, just like I predicted. No . . . he ain't the smartest boy on God's green earth. And no one sober would call him pretty. But he does okay."

She squinted, jiggling her hand as if to prod the eye into revealing more. The eye danced before coming still again.

"What I see now is the boy closing in on becom-ing a man. Thirteen he be. Ain't the luckiest of numbers, as you know. And for Norbert, thirteen is the worst. For that's when — " She stopped.

"What?" boomed the Mean One. "What?"

"Love," Zenith answered matter-of-factly. "Yep. Love's what I see. The boy is head over heels in love. Smitten he be. I see the face of a girl. Pretty enough. Dainty as a doily, with the temper of a bobcat lying just beneath the surface."

"I never liked girls. Nor bobcats," the Mean One interrupted.

"Hush yourself and let the woman speak," Maw said.

Zenith made the eye dance again. Gregory leaned closer, as if he, too, could see the images the woman foretold.

"Well," Zenith continued, "I see the boy at home. He's working on something. Workin' hard.

Cutting and humming and singing and pasting something special. Can't see what it be. He's guarding it too close. Even Clyde and Dolores can't sneak a peek of what the boy is working on." She paused for only an instant. "There!" she said, her voice rising shrill. "There, now. The thing is finished. And Norbert is happy as a boy can be."

"Bet it's a gift," Maw said. "A gift for the girl."

Zenith clamped her fingers around the eye quick as one of them meat-eating plants closing its jaws round a fly.

"Now, look here," she told Maw. "If'n you want to be the one reading the future, you can pluck out your own eye and read away. Won't faze me in the least."

Maw had a notion to get huffy herself. But thought better of it. "I'll keep my eyes where they be," she said by way of an apology.

"Good," said Zenith. "Now, where was I?" She opened her hand, the painted circle of iris staring back at her. "Oh, yes," she said. "The special something is a gift. A gift for the girl. I can see a calendar tacked to the cabin wall. Turned to February, is the calendar. And one of the dates is circled. Yep. The fourteenth . . . that's the date Norbert has circled with his own hand."

"Valentine's Day!" Gregory shouted.

"I was gonna say that," Zenith snapped.

"And now I see Norbert on the day itself. Blood bubbling happily through his young veins. Carrying a gift under his shirt to school. All is grand. . . . No, wait!" she hollered, causing all three listeners to jump at the same time. "All is not so grand. Storm clouds brewin'. A slew of 'em. And it won't be good for Norbert. No, not by a long shot. Sadness it be. And tears . . . tears for lots of folks from that day onward. And — "

"And what?" Gregory said, barely breathing.

"And that's as far as I go," said Zenith, breaking out of her trance. In a move both swift and sure, she popped the eye back into its hole, giving it a squeaky half turn to make sure it'd stay.

"I never divulge the bad," she said after snapping back the patch. "Wouldn't be in business for long if I did. It's the good that folks want to hear. I can point 'em to the bad, but it's them who have to face it if they've a mind to." She glared at the Mean One.

"She's right," Maw said. "It's why we come here in the first place. Least we know the time and place to find what we're after." She nodded forcefully. "Yessir . . . it's thirteen years into the future we're to be heading. To the Flat Rock schoolhouse on Valentine's Day. Thanks, Zenith. You've been a real eye opener."

"I ain't going," the Mean One burst. "I hate school. Hate school and the little vermin that go there." He stared crinkly-eyed at Gregory, as if the boy were an ant soon to be flattened.

"But Maw," said Gregory, unhitching his eyes

from the Mean One and tapping his pocket. "I only got but two peppers left. Just enough to get us back to Sharpesville. If we use 'em for another stop-over, we might be stranded forever."

A shiver rippled Maw's feathers at the thought.

Zenith shrugged, figuring she'd done all in her power to help.

It was exactly then that Gregory noticed streaks of color and light coming from behind the caravan. Thinking such a sudden display of light could mean only one thing, he yelled, "Maw! Zenith! Fire!"

Maw was on the wing at once. Gregory not far behind. What they saw when they rounded the caravan was a sight few have seen. The compost heap was aflame. Aflame with blue, green, and yellow sparks that shuddered silently, bursting out from deep within the pile.

Mesmerized by the tiny sputtering flames, Gregory approached, expecting to feel the heat rush against him. What he found was the opposite. The fire burned cool, a refreshing breeze whiffling over him, the air suddenly rid of its garbage smell altogether.

"I heard of such a thing," Maw said. "Saw the likes of it once in Paducah at a field that was freshly plowed under. Thought my eyes were playing tricks on me."

"Foxfire!" Zenith cried, rounding the caravan a step in front of the Mean One. "Said you'd need a bit of luck." She shook the bones in her pocket.

"There be your luck. Foxfire! Rare as a two-headed calf. Ain't real fire at all. It's the garbage churnin' itself into new life . . . the past changing to the future. Folks around here call it the door to the future."

"I don't see no door," said the Mean One.

"Not a real *door* door," Zenith spat in disgust.

"No," said Maw. "Ain't that kind of door. But it's just the kind we be needin'. What we're seeing is opportunity staring us in the face. That settles it, then. We're going through."

"Can't promise you'll get to the future time you're after," Zenith replied. "Might end up in next week, or next year, or a hundred years from now."

"No we won't," Gregory said, jamming his hand into his pocket and pulling out Sy's watch. "We can just set the sums of the proper date same as before."

Maw avowed that Gregory had a head full of brain. She told the Mean One to hurry and fetch Killer, 'cause his heart was waiting. Then she and Gregory worked on the sums, adding $2 + 14 + 95$ all the way down to 3.

Gregory set the watch for three o'clock just as the Mean One returned with Killer. They mounted up quickly.

Zenith took the pitchfork and spread the fire around, keeping her toes clear of the flames. "I'd go to the future with y'all," she said. "But at my age I might find myself dead."

Killer bucked apprehensively. Gregory used his hands to cover the horse's eyes so Killer wouldn't have to see what he was about to step through.

"If I *am* still kicking in thirteen years," Zenith said, "I'll be hightailin' it out of this place on the day you're aimin' for. Won't be hardly safe for an old lady like me on that day. So we best say our good-byes."

They did. Then Gregory's heels jolted Killer forward. Blindly, the horse trotted into the fire, his head disappearing first. Zenith watched as Gregory, Maw, and the Mean One dissolved one at a time into nothingness. Her final sight was of Killer's tail, swishing two or three times all by itself. Then it, too, was gone.

Zenith's scalp tingled. She felt the goose bumps sprout from her toes. Better to just tell the future than to jump into it, she told herself. Safer.

12. Clotheslines & Crawdads

It was something, the way the dark rolled over on itself soon as Killer entered the flames. Suddenly it was light. A white, bright, noonday light that caused all three riders to nearly blink themselves silly. When their eyes adjusted, they couldn't believe what they saw. Maw said later it was like the whole state of Kentucky had picked the same day to do their laundry.

What was stretched out row upon row before them were clotheslines. That's right . . . clotheslines. The lines were hung with bedsheets. Hundreds of sheets, put out to dry. Shoulder to shoulder they hung. So close together you couldn't see nothing but cloth. Wall upon wall of sheet cloth dancing and snapping in the air.

There was barely time to take in the sight before the first wall of sheets came charging. Being up front, Gregory and Maw were the first to be struck. The sheets hit them square in the faces, the cloth wet and soft and molding itself to the highs and lows of their features. The two feared the cloth might plug up their breathing holes for good, suffocating them right there on the spot. But it didn't happen that way. For the sheets were moving much too fast to stick for long. And in a trice, the cloth brushed clear, moving past to strike the Mean One, whose look of utter astonishment was quickly captured the way the face of a dead Egyptian shows through its mummy wrap.

Scritch went the sheets, sliding over their skin. *Oooh*, they said. Then another and another. *Scritch . . . Oooh. Scritch . . . Oooh . . . Scritch . . . Argh!* (That last from the Mean One, who remained as contrary in the future as he'd been in the past.) Like huge tongues, those sheets. All licky and tickly. Combing back feathers, hair, and lashes . . . wet and soft and cool as mountain air. Thirteen lines of sheets. Thirteen years washed away. Just that quick. Until the snapping and flapping and scritching stopped.

Maw was the first to find her voice. "Why, we ain't moved at all," she cried.

She was right. They hadn't moved but a yard or two. Killer stood ankle deep in some of the finest, blackest soil Gregory had ever seen. They were smack-dab in the center of Zenith's old compost heap. But the garbage was long decomposed. And not a spark of foxfire to be seen.

"Sheets!" said Gregory. "Did you see 'em, Maw? Tons of 'em. Who would believe it?"

Maw ran a wing over her scritched-down head feathers. "Believe it," she said.

In fact, they were all combed and scritched to a sheen. You could have looked all day through Killer's mane and tail and not spotted a single burr.

The Mean One's whiskers had been picked free of every moldering fish bone and catsup splorch. "Y'all weren't looking," he said with bravado. "But I killed plenty of them sheets. *Argh!*" he added, mussing his straightened whiskers to their former disarray.

Around them was a low picket fence with signs posted every few feet, warning *No Trespassin' for Thirteen Years.*

"Zenith watched over us," Gregory said.

He looked to where the caravan had once stood, fearing he might see a grave marker. But there wasn't a marker in sight. Only something piled just outside the fence. Gregory quickly slid himself off Killer and ran to the mysterious pile.

"Rattlesnake knuckles!" he called out. "And a note."

It was a note, all right. Written on a thick strip of tree bark. "Good luck," it said. "I ain't dead yet. And I don't plan to be. So I'm pulling out. Happy Valentine's Day."

"Valentine's Day!" Maw said, looking to the east, where the sun had already risen. "And if we don't hurry we'll be late for school."

Then — with the Mean One restating his hatred for school and loudly informing everything within earshot that time was running out for Gregory and Maw and that in only a few hours the both of them would be his to stomp or shred as he pleased — they left Zenith's old homesite behind and followed the sloping path to the main road. There Maw pointed a wing toward Flat Rock. She had a notion to go the other way and pay a visit to Clyde and Dolores, but she figured such a visit would only serve to upset Norbert on his big day.

So they headed straight for town instead, Gregory flicking the reins, his insides throbbing with excitement over what was to come. You couldn't blame Gregory for feeling such. For they were going to school. To the schoolhouse on Valentine's Day. The day the Mean One lost his heart and all heck broke loose.

*   *   *

If Maw *had* followed through on her notion to visit the Meaney cabin, she would have found things to be about the same. Except for Norbert. At thirteen, Norbert stood as tall and strapping as his daddy. The boy was strong as an ox. As ungainly, too — his knees and elbows tending to have lives of their own and knocking over whatever wasn't nailed down.

Norbert had never woke happier than he did that morning. He ate breakfast with his ma and pa, humming up a storm. Clyde and Dolores gave each other knowing looks across the table. They suspected their boy had been bitten by the love bug. (Parents have a way of knowing such things.) And they were glad for it, since Norbert, despite his good points, was as skittish as a deer on ice when it came to girls.

"Special day?" Clyde asked as the boy slurped up the last of his eggs.

Norbert's knees rapped the table, lifting it a little, his milk tumbling over. "Very special," he said.

Dolores smiled, nodding to her husband. She wondered what Norbert had been secretly working on for so long, but was aware of the boy's need for privacy and refused to pry.

Norbert splashed his face with water at the washbowl and used a horse brush to straighten the dark fuzz on his chin. The fuzz was growing thicker by the day. He had a right nice beard going.

From his bunk, Norbert told his parents they'd no need to be looking just now. Clyde and Dolores turned their heads respectfully, allowing Norbert to tuck his special something under his shirt. Before closing up the shirt, he drew out the valentine for another look. The big valentine was made from the best oiled paper, colored gold as a cat's eye. The heart was edged all around by a linen border painstakingly cut in half moons, which he'd sewn on with care. In the center, surrounded by an inner heart of lace, was a poem.

Norbert softly read the words he'd struggled with for so long.

Embarrassed at having written such a romantic poem, he stashed the heart inside his shirt and buttoned it safe. Then he quickly grabbed his lunch sack from the sideboard. He'd made the lunch himself the night before. Inside the sack were two sandwiches. He hoped to share one with Becky after giving her his heart. He'd caught himself a pair of crawdads — big as his fists — down by the creek. And had steamed them up perfect with the shells still on, so they'd be nice and crunchy, before laying them between slices of Dolores's bread.

Hurrying for the door, Norbert threw his parents kisses. Normally, he'd kiss his ma and pa proper before going off to school. But not today. Today he was saving his lips for Becky.

13. Fiddlesticks

Gregory pulled Killer to a stop at the head of town. Maw advised a still-grumbling Mean One to lower the straw hat over his face so no one would mistake him for Clyde or think Iris and the circus had rolled into town. Though the day was still new, dark clouds cooked ominous to the north.

"Storm clouds," Gregory said, recalling Zenith's prediction.

Maw breathed deep. She knew foreshadowing when she saw it but remained resolute. "A task once started needs finishing," she said. "Let's mosey."

And mosey they did. Heading for the schoolhouse. Following the town's children, who popped out of doors and alleyways with books tucked under their arms. When Maw remarked how Flat Rock had grown some over the years, Gregory had to agree. "Miss Lucy sure done all right by herself," he said.

Indeed, Miss Lucy had expanded her operations. The shop now took up the first floor of an entire building. A cute and sassy flower-print canopy stretched along the length of the shop. Hung from the canopy was a spanking-new sign that said, *Miss Lucy's Hefty Fashions & Awning Company.*

Curious about Samuel, Gregory asked a passing couple as to the undertaker's whereabouts.

"Far as I know Samuel Deeter's preaching over in Prickly Valley," the man said. "He embraced the cloth some years back. Swindled some strangers for a burial, then saw a ghost, which he took to be a sign that he'd best change his ways. He comes around now and again to visit his wife. She's the one that took over the business. Gemma LouAnn's her name."

The man waved a hand toward a second-story window whose black lettering read, *G.L.A.D. Undertaking.*

"You need to bury someone?" the woman added. " 'Cause I can vouch for Gemma LouAnn. She's got a green thumb when it comes to plantin' folks."

"No," said Gregory. "Leastways, I hope we don't have to do any burying. But thanks anyhow."

The schoolhouse stood just outside the town proper. It was a narrow building with tall windows. A big old juniper tree stood to one side, its thick greenery reaching all the way to the steepled roof.

For all his former bravado, the Mean One bristled like a scairt porcupine when he saw the school.

"I'm sick," he said. "It hurts here and here and here."

Maw wasn't buying it. "I ain't writing no excuses to the teacher the very first day," she said.

The yard was abuzz with talk of who loved who. It was Valentine's Day, after all, and the children had gussied themselves up for the event. Everyone looked well scrubbed from sponge baths the night before. The girls wore party dresses, all crinkly and lacy — their hair falling in thick ringlets over their shoulders. Some could be seen pinching their cheeks so the color would rise and cause them to be even prettier. "Lunchtime at the meetin' tree," they whispered to one another between fits of giggles, their eyes turning toward the boys.

Standing together in clumps, the boys boxed each other's ears in nervous anticipation. From time to time they'd spit in their hands, using the wet to slap down stubborn cowlicks. Those who wore shoes wobbled first on one foot then the other, polishing the leather against their trousers. "Lunchtime," they kept saying, their eyes darting toward the girls. "At the meetin' tree."

The children were all so busy primping and carrying on, they hardly took notice as Gregory led Killer to the school's hitchin' post. Slinging himself off, Gregory tied the horse to the post. Maw came right out and asked a chubby boy standing nearby about lunchtime at the meetin' tree. Surprised, the boy lifted his hand from his head, his cowlick springing up. He smiled crookedly at Gregory.

"You can't fool me," he said. "You're one of them ventriloquist people . . . throwing your voice so the bird there appears to speak. You're new here, ain't ya?"

Gregory admitted it'd been a few years since he'd last paid a visit to Flat Rock. The boy seemed eager to fill him in. "You're looking at the meetin' tree," he said, pointing to the juniper. "Come lunch, anyone can step under the tree, and whoever has a valentine for that person has to give it to them in front of *everyone*." His eyes widened with the thought. Then closed fast when he got his ears boxed from behind. "I'll knock you silly!" he cried, taking off after the attacker with fists extended.

It didn't take Maw long to size up the situation. "You're not going to school after all," she told the Mean One.

"I'm not? You mean I can tear the place apart one board at a time and chase all those little vermin until their legs fall off?"

"You'll do no such thing. What you'll do is git yourself up that tree and lie low — or in this case, high — until lunchtime. From the sound of it, that's when things'll be happenin'. And the tree will offer you a view of the action."

"Good idea, Maw," Gregory said. "He'd stick out like a hammered thumb in school. No telling what the teacher would say."

Maw nodded. The Mean One looked daggers at first her, then Gregory. Cursing under his breath, he slung himself off Killer and plodded for the tree. His chest hurt awful, but he was mean enough to wish things wouldn't work out — despite the pain — just so he could take his revenge on the both of them.

Awkward as a cow, the Mean One climbed into the branches with Maw and Gregory shouting, "Higher!" until there was nothing to be seen but the bottoms of his boots.

When Gregory turned back to the school yard, he said, "Look, Maw!"

There certainly was no mistaking Norbert. Taller than most men, the boy bounced up to the yard with head held high.

"He looks right handsome," Gregory said.

"Shows just how powerful a potion love is," Maw replied. "Only something as strong as love could turn a face like that respectable."

Suddenly the teacher, Mrs. Applebee, burst from the building with a big cowbell in hand. She gave the bell a good three shakes. The children stopped their playing and filed in behind her, chittering like squirrels, the boys getting in a last few licks and taunts. Gregory filed in, too, with Maw on his shoulder, thinking it might be fun to enroll in school in Sharpesville come September if he lived that long.

"You got yourself a crow there," Norbert said when Gregory squiggled in beside him on the seat bench farthest back.

"Yes, I have," Gregory replied.

Norbert smiled. But Gregory didn't feel the smile was for him. In fact, Norbert's gaze had slipped from Gregory to the far end of the bench, where two girls sat, readying their slates and whispering.

Mrs. Applebee finished calling roll and looked to the back. "Appears we have a new face here today," she said, studying on Gregory. "And who might you be?"

"Gregory, ma'am," Gregory said, standing up.

There were gasps and murmurs and pointing fingers, then, as the children got their first real look at Maw. Mrs. Applebee was no less surprised. "Is that a — ?"

"Crow, ma'am . . . yes, it is."

"Is it stuffed?"

"No, ma'am. We didn't have a chance to eat breakfast this morning."

Mrs. Applebee worked her mouth from side to side.

"I'm sorry to say this, Gregory, but pets aren't allowed at school."

"But ma'am," Gregory said, "Maw's more than

smart enough to be in school. Why, she taught me 'most everything I know. If I prove how smart she is, can she stay? Just for this mornin'?"

The other children were glad for any delay in starting their lessons. Plus they were interested to see just how smart a bird could be. "Yes!" they shouted, clapping and jumping in their seats. "Please, Mrs. Applebee. Pleeeease!"

"Well, it certainly is unusual," the teacher said. "But I'm always willing to discover something new. That's what we're here for. Right, children?"

"Oh, yes . . . yes!" the children responded.

She smiled. "Go ahead, then, Gregory. Prove away."

Gregory looked to the front board. There were sums written there, and he chose the hardest one. "See that sum up there?" he told Maw. "It says six plus seven. What's six plus seven, Maw?"

The room went instantly quiet as the children started counting on their fingers. Maw bit her tongue to keep from blurting out the answer. She figured if there was a rule against pets, there was most likely an even stricter one against crows who could talk, and she had no desire to push Mrs. Applebee over the edge. (The woman appeared the tetchy type.)

Still, Maw considered it an insult to be given such an easy sum. And she bobbed and nodded to Gregory that if the Mean One weren't even then peering in at them through the branches of the juniper, bent on destroying everything in sight if he didn't find his heart — well, she'd stomp right out of the place like the self-respecting crow she was.

Having aired her feelings, she suddenly aired her wings. The children ducked, drawing in their breaths. Maw landed right atop Mrs. Applebee's desk, causing the teacher to take a step back and give a little shriek at the same time. With a roll of her eyes, Maw stepped up to the cowbell and quickly pecked out the answer — the bell chiming with each peck. Thirteen pecks and thirteen chimes.

Stunned, Mrs. Applebee asked the children if Maw was right.

Norbert's hand shot up. "I had to use three of my toes," he said. "But I got the same answer . . . thirteen."

"You're both right," Mrs. Applebee said, truly delighted. "Six plus seven is thirteen. And the bird can stay. It will add to the specialness of our day." She smiled. "Because what day is it, children?"

"VALENTINE'S DAY!" the children yelled.

As the lessons progressed, it didn't take long for Gregory to figure who Norbert was sweet on. It was the girl at the far end of the bench. Her name was Becky. Her hair was spun into golden ringlets that she kept patting lightly just to feel their fullness. Her yellow dress crinkled like dry grass whenever she stood to answer a question, the smell of honeysuckle wafting thick down the bench.

It was during grammar, when Mrs. Applebee

was explaining the difference between *cain't* and *can't*, that Norbert gave his slate to Gregory, whispering for him to pass it on to Becky. On the slate was written, *Do you like crawdads?*

The slate got passed back in a hurry. *Only if they come from you* was Becky's answer.

Norbert sighed loudly. Becky sighed just as loud in reply. Maw told Gregory she hadn't seen this much honey slung around since she'd watched a bear take apart a bee's nest in the old oak she used to frequent in Paducah.

At midmorning, there was a five-minute recess for the children to stretch. Gregory took the opportunity to run outside and check on the Mean One. Maw would have liked to join him, but she was besieged by admiring students who kept giving her sums to solve.

"NO!" the Mean One bellowed down to Gregory. "I ain't okay at all. I'm cramped up stiff and my chest is killin' me."

In frustration, he gave the tree a mighty shake, the topmost branches swinging wildly and releasing a hailstorm of juniper berries that plunked off Gregory's head like hardened peas.

"And there's a bird, too," the Mean One roared again. "Keeps makin' passes at my beard. If I catch it, I'm gonna wring its neck and give it to Killer for pulverizin'. . . . "

Gregory could see there was no stopping the man's grumping, and he dashed back to school before another volley of berries could reach him.

Just inside the school's entranceway was a narrow little coatroom. Passing it, Gregory heard laughter. He poked his head in, curious, and saw three boys huddled together around one of the lunch sacks. He heard a sound he couldn't place. Like an unoiled door, or a belch signifying gastric distress. The boys pulled apart soon as they saw him.

"What do *you* want?" one of the boys growled.

"Nothing much," Gregory said. "Just tryin' to be friendly. Don't believe I caught your name when we was learnin' this morning."

"Fiddlesticks!" the boy answered, making fists of his hands. "Wanna make sumpin' of it?"

"Nope," said Gregory. "Cain't see nothing to be made of a person's name."

The boy gave a sneer. Gregory shrugged and left, thinking the boy was unkindly 'cause he didn't like being named Fiddlesticks. He couldn't blame him, really.

Mrs. Applebee had a tough time keeping the children's attention the rest of the morning. It was the valentine exchange at the meetin' tree that filled the children's minds more than how to loop their p's and q's. Between Norbert's huge sighs and Becky's wafts of honeysuckle that traveled like smoke signals down the bench, Gregory could hardly think at all. Maw kept coughing like she had the croup, fanning her wings just to keep the air moving. When the long-awaited lunchtime rolled around, it was as if Mrs. Applebee had said *"Fire!"* instead of *"Dismissed."*

14. Madman

Valentines clutched in their sweaty palms, the children thronged around the tree. "Who'll be first? Who'll be first?" they cried, their voices rising to the dark clouds that looked like burnt biscuits overhead.

Both Maw and Gregory knew this was it. Hazarding a look up into the tree, they saw the whites of the Mean One's eyes staring back at them through the green. Maw only wished she had a few of Zenith's rattlesnake bones to shake. Gregory clacked one set of molars against the other, sounding like a jittery telegraph key.

How the exchange worked was like this: First a girl would step under the tree. Then whatever boy had a valentine for her, that boy would step up and give it. If two or more boys moved forward, the girl would point the order of how she wished to receive them, saving the one she liked most for last. The best that could happen was if a girl and a boy had each made valentines for the other . . . if the liking was mutual. Then the children would chant, "True love! True love!" And the two had to kiss right there in front of everyone.

It was, of course, the promise of kissing that had the children giggling and kicking the dirt and generally all giddy with excitement.

One by one the girls stepped forward. Finally, it was Becky's turn. Norbert lunged ahead so fast, he tripped over an exposed root and fell. He picked himself up, though, too intent on his sweetie to be bothered by the laughter.

"Wait!" came a voice. "I got one for Becky, too."

Gregory was surprised to see Fiddlesticks emerge from the crowd.

Becky beamed to discover herself in demand. "Now, let's see . . ." she said, tapping a finger to her chin. But she was only play-acting. And after milking the tension for all it was worth, she pointed to Fiddlesticks to go first.

"Aren't you gonna save me for last?" Fiddlesticks said angrily.

Indeed, Becky wasn't. She turned her loving gaze to Norbert, who tripped at the sight of it even though he was standing still.

"Then I ain't givin' you nothin'," Fiddlesticks shot. "You'll find out just how much the big ox loves you. You'll find out for sure!" With that he stepped back, elbowing his pals, the three snickering like coyotes who discover the henhouse door left open.

"They did something!" Gregory whispered hard to Maw. "I saw 'em earlier messin' with the lunches."

Maw stiffened. "Never expected this to be a picnic," she said.

No magician ever received more *oohs* and *aahs* than did Norbert when he pulled the gold heart from his shirt and shakily gave it to Becky. It was surely the biggest valentine anyone had ever seen. The most elaborate, too, with its half-moon linen border and inner heart of lace around which the boy's poem was written.

"What's it say?" the children clamored. "What's it say?"

Becky touched her gold ringlets, then read aloud, turning the heart to follow the words. "Roses are red," she said. "Violets are blue. Looking at you . . . Makes me so cu-ckoo."

Several girls swooned.

"He's a poet," said one, fanning the heat from her forehead.

"That's *so* sweet," said another, hands cupped to her face.

When Becky took out her own valentine and handed it to Norbert, the children went crazy. "True love! True love!" they chanted.

Maybe it was then that the Mean One's memory was finally unblocked. Maybe then he knew what was coming. For at that very moment Gregory thought he heard a horrible moan give out from the tree. It was hard to tell for sure, since the wind had picked up to a shirt-billowing whirl, the burnt-biscuit clouds above slamming into one another with the onrushing air. And when Becky and Norbert kissed, the sky burst with thunder and lit up with a fork of lightning that seared the eyeballs of everyone present.

Norbert and Becky pulled their lips apart at the same time, their faces redder than a smoke-filled sunset.

"Wow," someone said.

The rain fell in the tiniest droplets at first, kinda slow and indecisive. Then increased. Norbert hardly noticed as he picked up his lunch sack and held it open for Becky. "Made a sandwich special," he said, his lips still atingle. "Just for you."

Dainty as a doily, her own lips likewise atingle, Becky reached into the sack. Her face screwed into a question at what she touched. She'd never known a sandwich to be so smooth and moist and veiny and . . . "Alive!" she screamed.

A frog, the biggest bullfrog Gregory had ever laid eyes on, leaped suddenly out of the sack, latching its grippy fingers to Becky's face — expressing its delight at being set free with a full-throated croak and a blink of its enormous eyes.

Fiddlesticks and his pals were the first to burst

out laughing. Then the others joined in. Becky screamed again, her breath tickling the frog's underbelly. Tickled him right off her face and onto her head, where the frog seemed to find her golden ringlets softer than any lily pad.

Becky's lips were more aquiver than atingle by this time. "Get it off me!" she yelled. "Get — it — off!"

Shocked, Norbert lunged for the frog. With another throaty croak, the frog jumped again. A short jaunt this time. To the back of Becky's neck. There to begin its search for a safe place to hide from all the screeching and laughter. It found such a place, too. Nosed its way right under poor Becky's collar, exhaling its bulk thin and slipping into the dark under her dress.

Well, it was like the exchange had turned into a hoedown.

"The girl can move," Maw said as Becky cavorted. It was a new dance, high-stepping and full of frenzied abandon, punctuated by yells and hands slap-grabbing at her dress.

With a crinkling of crinoline, the frog finally dropped to the ground. Dazed by so much honeysuckle, its great eyes circled around its head as though following the buzz of a mosquito that wasn't there.

One of the younger children couldn't help feeling sorry for the critter. "It's all shook up," the girl said. And she ran to offer her condolences, but the frog recovered quick enough to take three giant hops and find shelter and sanity in the nearby hedge.

By now the other children were mostly on the ground, limp with laughter and soggy with rainwater.

"You beast!" Becky fired at Norbert. "I hate you! And this is what I think of your heart!"

"No!" cried Norbert.

"No!" came a resounding echo from the branches above.

Holding Norbert's heart out, Becky ripped once, then twice, then a third, fourth, and fifth time. She flung the shredded pieces to the air, where the wind blew them like confetti, sending them in every direction.

"My heart!" said Norbert.

"MY HEART!" boomed the Mean One, thrashing so hard in his perch that the children were hit with a barrage of juniper berries. Looking up, the children felt their own hearts turn to ice at what they saw.

"A madman!" they shouted. "Look . . . up there! A madman!"

Fiddlesticks and his pals were among the first to run off toward the schoolhouse, hollering for Mrs. Applebee to save them.

Maw and Gregory had sprung into action soon as Becky released Norbert's heart to the wind. Maw loop-de-looped herself like never before, swerving and diving in an attempt to catch hold of the skittering pieces. Gregory ran helter-skelter, leaping, gyrating, reaching out to capture the elusive scraps. But the wind, added to by the Mean One's thrashing, made sport of their attempts. They might just as well have tried catching the fleas from a hound's porch blanket in a summer gale.

"Where?" Mrs. Applebee yelled, rushing up. "Where, children?"

When she saw the wild man above — arms and legs splayed out . . . grrring and roaring — she offered a prayer, saying, "Save us all." Then, "Inside, children! All of you . . . quick!"

The children charged in a mass toward school. All but Norbert, who stood stunned and broken, watching the pieces of his heart scatter like snow.

"It's no use," Maw said, spitting out a beakful of juniper bark and shaking her head after trying unsuccessfully to spear a scrap of the heart.

Exhausted by his own vain pursuits, Gregory said, "Maw. Look. The townsfolk are coming!"

They were, too. Having heard the screams of their children, the people of Flat Rock came running for the school, yelling *"Tarnation"* and *"Madman"* and *"Our babies!"*

Through the rain Gregory saw a glint of silver. "We'll be arrested, Maw. There's a sheriff among 'em."

Killer reared at the word, jerking himself free from the hitchin' post. Gregory grabbed the loose reins before the horse could set his peepers on the oncoming badge and wrestled him to the tree.

"Jump!" Gregory called to the Mean One. "JUMP!"

"You said you'd give me back my heart," the Mean One replied. "I ain't jumpin'."

He didn't jump. But he did come down. In his anger, he gave the tree such a shaking that the limb he was on cracked like a stick of peppermint candy, sending the giant down in a flurry of twigs and needles. He landed on Killer with such force that the horse gave out an *Oomph*, its feet sinking a good three inches into the ground with the weight.

"Mount up!" Maw told Gregory. "We're outta here!"

Gregory scrambled up, positioning himself in front of the Mean One. Maw was clinging to the boy's shoulder a second later. "Rotten luck," she said, "that heart gettin' blown away like that."

The Mean One moaned and swayed at the mention of it. Gregory wrapped the man's arms around his waist to prevent the big guy from falling off for good.

"The peppers!" Maw crowed, coming out of her reverie as the townsfolk closed in.

Tearing the peppers from his pocket, Gregory shoved them toward Killer. "Peppers, boy . . . remember?"

Killer remembered, all right. Just the smell of

them fire-breathing-dragon chilis made him leap. When he came down, he looked over his shoulder at Gregory's hand just to be sure he wasn't having another nightmare.

Gregory pushed the peppers closer to the horse's head. "See 'em, boy? They're coming to git ya!"

Not about to let the peppers come an inch closer, Killer's weight rippled to his back legs as he prepared to launch.

"Hey, youse . . . stop!" came the shouts of the townsfolk as they reached the yard.

"Hang on, Maw," Gregory yelled.

"North!" screamed Maw. "To Sharpesville!"

If they had stayed a moment longer, they would have seen Norbert come out of his stupor. For the boy *did* fin'ly move. Not far. Just a step. To his lunch that lay soaked and muddied on the ground. There he stomped the dead crawdads even deader.

Having taken this first step, the rest was easy. Reaching down, Norbert picked up a rock big as a cantaloupe. This he held up, threatening the townsfolk, who stopped when they saw the wild in his eyes.

Turning, Norbert fixed his steely gaze on the children who watched terror-stricken out the school window with Mrs. Applebee. And recalling the laughter . . . the loss . . . the terrible day he was having, the boy made his decision — a decision that would affect so many for so long. Putting all his weight into it, Norbert let the rock fly. The children and teacher were just able to scatter before the window was smashed to smithereens.

You would think this would've been enough. But it wasn't. Norbert then cleared a ball of phlegm from his throat and spat it toward Flat Rock's sheriff . . . the jellylike awfulness falling just short of the man's boots.

The sheriff shook his head and clicked his tongue.

"He's a mean one," he pronounced.

And that, as they say, was that.

15. A Hearty Ending

Killer skipped *FAST*er altogether. Went from *F*ast to *FASTEST!* requiring only *two* shakes of a squirrel's tail instead of the three as before. Wasn't just the threat of peppers spurring him on. Once a horse gets a sniff of home, there's no measuring its speed.

Funniest thing was, for the people of Sharpesville only seconds had passed. Even as Gregory and Maw and the Mean One were making their way back, the citizens of Sharpesville stood where they had . . . in the center of Main Street, looking south to where the dust still churned against the horizon.

There was Sy . . . still clinging to the single

strand of what had once been his made-in-Paris toupee.

And Amos, breathing heavy, having only just joined the others after releasing Bullet.

In her rocker sat Thelma — the taste of *Ride 'im cowboy* still on her lips — thinking that's the way she wanted to go when the Almighty called her. Not on a horse, mind you. But fast.

Victoria — all squeaked out — stood beside Millie, who stood next to Marsh, who stood aside Fiona, who clutched Little Gert close, trying to comfort the child who sniffled sadly at the thought of never again seeing her pal Gregory.

So they stood. Quiet and amazed. 'Cept for Bullet, who bayed and yipped like there was no tomorrow.

In the end it was Bullet's yapping that made things right. For Gregory and Maw had forgotten to set Sy's watch to the proper day and year. Killer might have bypassed Sharpesville altogether if not for Bullet's yowling. The horse pulled up quick when he heard it. Stopped right there in the center of Main Street, only a yard or two from the crazed hound. Gregory barely had a chance to say, "We're back!" before all three riders went flying.

Maw, of course, had no problem finding herself airborne. Gregory's shirt and trousers, heated dry from the ride and baggy as ever, puffed full of air to slow his fall. The crowd sprayed themselves out to make room for the Mean One, who landed hard where he packed the most weight . . . that being his bottom.

"See, dumplin'?" Fiona told a relieved Little Gert. "Gregory decided not to go to that Flat Rock place after all. Here he is, same as ever."

"But we did go," said Gregory, the air *pffisting* from his clothes as he somersaulted himself to his feet.

"Why, you weren't gone long enough to snip a set of eyebrows," said Sy.

"And your watch worked perfect," Gregory told him, handing over the watch. "See? Still not runnin'."

"We was gone, all right," Maw said. "We seen things and done things." Worried, she looked to the Mean One, who rose slowly, rubbing the sting from his backside.

"The heart?" Marsh said. "Did you find it?"

Maw knew there'd be no right purpose served in lying about it. "We gave it our best shot," she said.

It was then, bless her soul, that Gertie, squirming in Fiona's arms, pointed to Gregory's bare feet. "What's that, Geggie?" the little girl asked.

Gregory felt the something stuck to the bottom of his foot for the first time. "Must be a stickweed," he said, lifting his leg.

But what Gregory saw when he looked at his foot wasn't a stickweed at all. It was a piece of oiled paper. Just a scrap. Gold colored, with a bit of scratchy lace hanging from it. A clump of dried mud glued the scrap to the bottom of his sole. Gregory peeled the paper off like a worn-out bandage.

"Why, there's writing on it," he said.

Everyone gathered round for a look. When Gregory and Maw saw what was written there, their faces lit up smiley like the satisfied customers featured on labels of Dr. Peabody's Famous Corn Remover.

"We found it!" Gregory yelled. "Gertie . . . you found the Mean One's heart!"

"That ain't no heart," the Mean One said gruffly, yanking the scrap from Gregory's fingers.

"Read it," Gregory urged the giant.

The Mean One read slow, sounding out the words. There were only two words, but the big guy wasn't much of a reader (having quit both school and books that day under the meetin' tree), and he had to struggle through.

"L-ovvv-ve . . . N-Nor-berrr-t."

"Yes!" said Gregory.

"Yep!" echoed Maw.

"Told you I was good at finding things," Gertie said.

"But I wanted a real heart," the Mean One said.

"And you'll have one," said Maw. "That there scrap of valentine represents the love you lost under the meetin' tree that day so long ago. Now that you got it back, it's all you need to grow yourself a ticker that'll fill the hurt in any chest, even one as big as yours."

The Mean One still appeared unsure. Gregory

took the scrap and slipped it under the man's shirt.

"What do you feel?"

A raggedy smile broke through the glum of the Mean One's face. "The pain," he said. "The indigestion . . . it's gone!"

"Bet your boots it's gone," said Maw. "And I think I hear something, too."

The Mean One cocked his head to listen, scratching a hand through his dark whiskers as he did so.

"I hear it," he cried sudden. "I do. It's tickin'. It's actual beatin'!"

Maw fluttered her wings proud. "Folks," she said, "this here be Norbert Meaney."

The townspeople had a hard time believing it wasn't the Mean One standing before them. All except Victoria, who, being a baton twirler, knew a good turn when she saw it. Victoria caught the ragged smile turning up the corners of the Mean One's hairy lips.

"Why, he *is* different," she squeaked. "By gosh, he *is!*"

"You mean I'm Norbert again?" said the Mean One, hope washing over him. "You mean I got m'self a heart?"

There was no mistaking the smile now. It turned even broader as the man contemplated the thought of having his own honest-to-goodness heart.

It was Millie who broke the townfolks' silence, saying, "Glad to meet ya, Norbert. Welcome to Sharpesville."

* * *

Well, there's not a whole lot more to tell. Norbert's first wish was to get himself a good bath, much to the delight of everyone present since they were all tired of breathing through their mouths. Marsh and Amos volunteered to scrub down Norbert in Sy's barrel tub. Took a while to scrape off the layers of dirt. But they did it. And afterward, Sy gave Norbert his first shave ever.

Then Norbert joined Gregory and Maw and Victoria for some huckleberry pie at Fiona's. Victoria mentioned she'd appreciate Norbert giving her some twirling lessons on the baton.

"I think Norbert's got a few things to take care of first," Maw said.

"I have," Norbert said contritely.

Gregory and Maw had already talked it over with him. Norbert was going to lay some flowers on Sheriff Zimm's four graves in Vicksburg for a start. Then he planned to repay several hotel owners for broken windows he'd been responsible for during his horse-heaving days.

When Norbert recounted his plan, Fiona said, "Don't forget Hulberton."

Norbert nodded. "You don't suppose the schoolmaster is still stuck up that chimney, do ya?"

"Better check," said Fiona. "And you need to

explain to them poor children just what direction it is that geese fly to in winter."

"And your folks," Gregory said. "You said they might be still alive."

"Far as I know, they left Flat Rock along with most everyone else just before me and Killer leveled the place."

"Poor Dolores," said Maw. "Such a fine woman. And Clyde . . . never saw a man so proud to be a daddy."

"I've been a real stinker," Norbert said.

"But you will come back, won't you?" Victoria squeaked. She felt kinda drawn to the handsome giant with the clean-shaven face.

"Soon as I can," said Norbert.

"Then I'll wait," said Victoria. "For the baton lessons, I mean," she added, suddenly embarrassed.

And so, with their bellies full of huckleberries and the sun guttering like a torch whose fuel is nearly spent, Gregory and Maw struck out for home. Passing the church, they saw Killer taking his fill of the newly planted zinnias, Fiona having insisted that the horse deserved a good supper in order to build up his strength for Norbert's journey.

"Might be hard for Killer to give up sheriffs," Gregory said, speaking low so as not to excite the animal.

"Worse than the Mean One givin' up tobacco,"

Maw said. "But they can manage it if they want."

As they left the town behind them, Gregory felt his toes sink soft into the familiar road dust of home. "Been a hot day," he said.

Maw laughed. "Almost too hot."

"We done fine, didn't we, Maw?"

"Real fine," said Maw. She was already looking forward to working on her nest come morning. Gregory had a pocketful of whiskers that Sy had given him after Norbert's shave, and Maw couldn't wait to weave the bristles in strong and pretty.

"You think Norbert will make good on his mistakes?" Gregory asked.

"He's got a lot better chance at it now that he has a heart," Maw answered.

Gregory agreed. He hummed, then, and Maw added a throaty tune of her own. When they came in sight of the cabin, Gregory kicked up his heels, and Maw circled the place four times, saying it hadn't changed a lick in twenty-five years.

Lying on his mattress that night, Gregory had a question that wouldn't go away.

"You know, Maw, I love you so. And Marsh and Sy and Millie and Gertie and — " He stopped, suddenly thinking of how the Mean One had given his love to Becky and ended up with a heart full of empty.

"Something eatin' at you, boy?" Maw said.

"Well . . . you suppose a person has to worry about loving too much? I mean, you suppose there's just so much loving, and if you use it up all at once — or spread it around too thin — you come up short?"

Atop her rafter, Maw felt a warmth of emotion.

"A body never has to worry about using up their love," she said. "The more you use, the more there is. The Mean One could have learned that way back if'n he'd dug deeper. You supposin' that when I go courtin' and you end up with brothers and sisters, I'll have to love you any less just 'cause there'll be more to give to?"

"I was sorta wonderin' that," said Gregory.

"Why, there'd be a bushelful more of love to go around for everybody. Life is like that."

Gregory sighed with the thought. "Life is grand, ain't it?" he said.

"That it is," said Maw.

"Glad you're my maw," said Gregory.

"Love you too," said Maw.

"To pieces?" Gregory asked with a laugh.

"To pieces," said Maw.

"Good night, then," said Gregory.

"Night, son."

And *that's* what happened, the day the Mean One rode into town.